# THE
# Seraphim's Song

Book 5 of The F.I.G. Mysteries

Barbara Casey

An Imprint of Gauthier Publications

1st Edition
Hungry Goat Press is an Imprint of Gauthier Publications
www.EATaBOOK.com

ISBN: 978-1-942314-84-4

Books in Series

*O Music, lead the way--*
*The stormy night is past,*
*Lift up our hearts to greet the day,*
*And the joy of things that last.*

-Henry Van Dyke

*Music in the soul can be heard by the universe.*

-Lao Tzu

# Prologue

The cave, one of many created over time within the steep, rocky outcrop overlooking the Yellow Sea, was unremarkable. From all appearances, it had been naturally carved into the cliff face by the dust storms that frequented this western coastal area of China and the ebb and flow of tides. The singular thing that set it apart from all of the other caves, though, was that its entrance, rather than facing the sea, opened to the north, perpendicular to the shore. Through the centuries, its entrance had shrunk and grown less noticeable as shrubs, wild grasses, and small trees native to the area—Viburnum davidii, dawn redwood, dallisgrass, and the small dove tree—took root in the yellow clay soil. The cave became more hidden and more forbidden.

People visiting the area took no notice. But those who lived there, and the generations who had come before them, knew of the dark secrets held within the cave. They had heard the frightening, eerie sounds coming from the jagged mouth of the misplaced opening, and some had even claimed to have seen the monster living within.

The fire-breathing pig dragon.

With its yellow elongated head and a snout that resembled a boar, the five claws—the pig dragon was to be believed; it was to be feared. In earlier dynasties, sacrificial blood offerings had been made to appease the dragon. In more recent times, however, the cave was called *jinzhi de*, or forbidden, and it was simply avoided.

At the start of the eighth century Song dynasty, many members of the Chinese gentry began to pursue antiquarian hobbies like collecting art that soon led to scholars and officials retrieving several ancient relics from archaeological sites throughout the country. Many of these finds, such as ancient ceremonial vessels, were then used in state rituals. Over the years, tens of thousands of discoveries had been made, inland as well as throughout certain regions bordering the Yellow Sea. As a result, interest in Chinese artifacts had escalated on an international scale.

Remarkably, the one area that had been ignored was the ancient Gansu province of the northwest region of China. An area bordering on the Yellow Sea and rumored to have been originally settled by gypsies, it was believed to be rich in antiquities hidden in the caves. It was also believed to be the home of the pig dragon. And no matter how much time had passed, how much society had advanced and the cities modernized, how many old traditions and beliefs had been forgotten, debunked, or replaced by new, the stories of the pig dragon persisted. No archaeologist would explore this area.

Until now.

The Chinese people who lived in the province grew concerned. They knew the stories. Stories of the pig dragon and the early travelers who had come before—and then suddenly left. Since the small team of archaeologists had started to dig near the cave, the *shāchén* or dust devils were increasing in number and severity. Just like before. The strange disquieting sounds that had been heard by the early travelers could now once again be heard coming from deep within the cave, and the low, vibrating hum grew audibly in strength to those who listened.

The old people who had lived in the area their entire lives believed the stories from the past. Stories that had been passed down from their ancestors, and before them, the ancients—the star gods and angels that came down from the sky. They knew—the pig dragon with its coiled serpent body was real. They knew the pig dragon had been awakened.

*A bird does not sing because he has the*

*answer to something,*

*he sings because he has a song.*

-Chinese Proverb

# CHAPTER 1

The boy, hardly a man, haphazardly dug with his trowel, jabbing at the ground and tossing dirt and debris in no particular direction, all the while observing those working nearby. It was a newly discovered archaeological site aptly called the Luoli Project in the ancient Gansu province of the northwest region of China. A pejorative term, the name "Luoli" in Chinese meant a scorning of the lifestyle of a wandering people. The fact that it was believed to have been the early home of gypsies that could be traced back as far as the Yuan Dynasty, sometime between the eleventh and twelfth centuries, even before they traveled into Europe, was what had drawn Milosh to the area. At least that is what he told Dr. Richard Stanwick, expert in Chinese antiquities and head of the project. With nowhere else to go, and the fact that he was a gypsy—the son of a Bandoleer—he had quickly been hired by Dr. Stanwick.

What Milosh didn't reveal when he first approached Dr. Stanwick about work was that he had been disowned by his family and forcefully removed from his *Kaulo Camio* tribe, or more commonly known as the black tribe. Since his birth, there had been the darkness concealing that point of light around his heart—a brown *chakra* rather than green. He had hurt other gypsies in spite of numerous attempts to change him—to remove the darkness. His ultimate sin and downfall, however, was that he had placed a curse on the daughter of the *choovihni*, the wise woman of the tribe who had inherited the exalted and envied position among gypsy women.

As her birthright, she and she alone had been given the responsibility to pass on the knowledge of the travelers to the ones with the gift who would follow. It was also her responsibility to maintain peace within the tribe and eliminate any bad or negative elements. Because of his repeated transgressions, the *kris*—a gypsy court of law—had ruled that *marime* be enforced and Milosh banned from his tribe. No matter how much Milosh argued and begged—and threatened, the ruling could not be changed. There were no other options.

Disgraced and filled with hate and anger, he left his tribe with only a few clothes and some personal items. He also took with him the book of curses he had stolen from the Bandoleer, his father, and the small glass jar with strands of baby hair and poisonous herbs he had used against the *choovihni's* daughter.

The baby hair belonged to Lyuba's daughter. It was what had given him the power to place a curse of death on the daughter, and he had almost succeeded. With his anger and hatred only growing with time, he vowed to get revenge against Lyuba, the *choovihni*. It was she who was responsible for his banishment. And it was she who would pay. This time he would use different poisons, stronger and more deadly. This time he wouldn't fail. As Milosh carelessly dug into the loose soil, these evil thoughts consumed him, and the darkness around his heart grew darker still.

Because it was a new site, the lack of funding had made it difficult to hire workers; security was lax, something

Milosh could take advantage of. As a gypsy, Milosh knew about the early travelers and how they had spent time near the Yellow Sea in China. The only reason he had come to this area was his dream of finding hidden ancient treasures in that area and specifically in the *jinzhi de* cave.

Milosh continued to watch until he knew he could slip into the cave unnoticed. It was there on previous searches that he had discovered strange artifacts that included broken pieces of old pottery, ancient tools, as well as stones with some sort of writing or symbols. Some were in the form of painted pictographs; others, carved petroglyphs and hieroglyphs. They seemed to reflect different cultures and different periods in time. All were ancient and, therefore, valuable.

Rather than turn them in to Dr. Stanwick for further examination, he smuggled them away in order to sell to tourists in the nearby town of Puli where the internationally known Yellow Sea Laboratory was located. He got paid very little for the excavation he did at the archaeology site, but he got a great deal of money for the artifacts.

"You need to be more careful with your digging, Milosh." Dr. Stanwick leaned over his recently-hired worker and gently moved the mound of dirt under Milosh's trowel with a small brush. As Milosh watched, Dr. Stanwick uncovered what appeared to be a small piece of pottery—a broken bowl perhaps—that displayed the painted remnants of a blue flower. This was significant because of the flower and in that the blue color had been preserved through the centuries.

Milosh recognized the flower immediately. It was the wolfsbane, commonly known as the monkshood or friar's cap among gypsies. It was a flower that was esteemed by the travelers because of its healing properties which could be used to reduce fever. If used improperly, however, it could be deadly. It was what Lyuba had poisoned him with to teach him a lesson when she learned of his transgression against her daughter. This was proof that gypsies had settled in the area as far as he was concerned.

"I will be more careful," said Milosh, trying to conceal his temper. The broken pottery had probably belonged to a *choovihni* many centuries ago—back to the beginning. Even then, the wise woman would have known how to use the monkshood, for she, like Lyuba, would have had the knowledge.

He watched his boss walk away with the find, resenting that he kept such a close eye on what he did. He suspected that the only reason he had been hired to begin with was because the Chinese workers would never go into the cave. Their silly superstitions about some mythical fire-breathing dragon prevented it. Milosh didn't have those superstitions. The cave didn't frighten him.

For now, they were digging in an area outside the cave's entrance, just beyond the shoreline of the Yellow Sea. It would only be a matter of time, though, before Dr. Stanwick would want to move the digging closer to the entrance and into the dark depths of the cave itself. And that is why he needed Milosh. But if Milosh was patient—and careful—he would be able to find most of the valuable artifacts before Stanwick sent his workers who were not Chinese or superstitious into the cave.

Later that evening, just after dark, Milosh left the site and returned to his trailer a short walk away. The cave had produced more artifacts which he had stashed in a cloth bag he kept hidden in his trousers. Most were small and similar to what he had found previously. There was one piece in particular, however, that was much larger and a great deal heavier than the other artifacts. He found it wedged in the rocks of the cave wall, and it took a great deal of effort to gouge it loose. It was also a strange shape—cylindrical—and it appeared to be intact.

Thickly encrusted with the yellow dirt that was prevalent in the area, he could barely make out markings. He banged the object against the edge of a counter, dislodging some of the dirt, and then carelessly scraped at the dirt with the tip of a knife creating a jagged scar in its hard surface. It appeared to be jade, or maybe even crystal, which would be highly unusual. Like some of the other things he had found, it had carved symbols. Pleased with his find, he tossed it along with the other artifacts in the cloth bag on the floor next to the front door. He would clean it in the morning before going to the site.

That night, as he lay in bed, he flipped through the pages of the Bandoleer's old book of curses. He had bent down the corners of several pages, marking them to study again. It had been so easy before when he stole the herbs he needed from Lyuba's hut as well as the strands of hair. This time he would have to find a place that sold herbs and buy them. They wouldn't be as fresh as those Lyuba used, but they would do. There was an apothecary in the town of Puli called the *Guang Zhe Ji* that sold natural herbs. He would go there the next day to get what he needed.

It started out as a dust devil, or what the Chinese called *shāchén*. Frequently occurring in this area, people were accustomed to seeing them. But this one was different. Rather than moving in any one direction and then turning into itself and weakening into nothingness, it seemed to meander around the mouth of the *jinzhi de* cave, keeping its strength, as though searching for something. Then, after several moments, the people working at the Luoli site observed it quickly moving away, gaining in strength, picking up more dust and small rocks in its path.

Milosh was still in bed when he was awakened by the low-pitched hum followed by a strong vibration. Not sure what it was, he opened the door of his trailer to look outside. When he did he was immediately covered in a blinding thick yellow dust and pelted by flying debris. Before he could slam the door closed, everything in his trailer was lifted into the air and thrown about as it was caught up in the angry, swirling wind. His body stinging from the air-born sand and stones, he ran back to his bed and pulled the covers over his head. Only after he no longer heard the hum or felt the vibration did he once again venture out from under the bed covers.

Everything inside the trailer was broken and in shambles, and covered in thick yellow dust. Outside, some of the siding on the rusted metal shell of the trailer was missing or had been ripped loose; the rest severely pit-marked by the force of the dust devil. But he didn't care; the trailer wasn't his anyway. It had been provided for him to use while he worked at the site.

Then he noticed—the bag of artifacts he had left by the front door the night before wasn't there. He looked under broken chairs, piles of dirty clothing, a tipped table, under his bed, behind the soiled worn sofa, even in the small built-in cabinet next to the sink, everywhere he could think of with no luck. Outside he had no better luck. The artifacts he had planned to take into town to sell were gone, including the big one. They had all simply disappeared.

Angry and feeling sorry for himself, Milosh stomped around, kicking things that had fallen to the floor, throwing things that were now broken or useless, in an attempt to find something to wear that wasn't covered in thick yellow dust. He had worked hard finding those artifacts and taken great risks not to get caught. He could have gotten a lot of money for them, especially that big one.

Once again his thoughts turned to the *choovihni* who was responsible for everything bad in his life. He could have been the next Bandoleer of his tribe. He would have been respected and feared. His name would have been known throughout all of the Romani tribes. Instead, he had been banished without a home to a life of wandering from place to place. And other gypsy tribes refused to have anything to do with him. Lyuba had made certain they knew. He would cause Lyuba much pain. He had almost succeeded before when he put a curse on her daughter. Now he knew more; he possessed more of the secrets. He wouldn't fail the next time.

The *chakra* around Milosh's heart grew even darker.

Far off in the distance, the dust devil continued to gather in strength, size, and speed as it moved in a south-southwest direction toward its destination. It would soon reach the west coast of Africa, and when it did, it would merge with a large weather system starting to make its way across the Atlantic Ocean. Already a category 1 hurricane, it had been given the name Luoli.

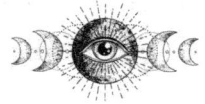

As she usually did in the early, pre-dawn hours, Lyuba was digging roots, in the dark of the crescent moon, and every so often replanting a good piece of a root to grow next year. The day before she had picked herbs, during that time when the essential oils are at their strongest, before they could get evaporated by the midday sun. Where she searched was her favorite place, the place where the energies were strongest. Surprisingly, it was the old church graveyard built on a slight mound just outside of the rural Italian village of Frascati, which is why the other gypsy women stayed away. Unlike Lyuba, they feared being so near the dead. They believed that being near death would hasten their own, therefore they refused to go there. Lyuba, however, saw death as the natural and necessary progression of life, in another form, in a different dimension. She found comfort and solace in its nearness.

A creek ran nearby, and a tall, unkempt yew tree

grew near the entrance to the graveyard; poisonous, but giving off positive energies. It was a place Lyuba knew well, having discovered it from earlier times when the travelers came this way. It was there where she found peace.

She would prepare her potions from the roots, bark, and hard seeds she gathered and make decoctions by soaking them overnight and boiling them the next day. Some of the decoctions she would add honey or sugar to; others she would thicken into syrup or add lard to make ointments and salves. The freshest herbs she saved for her oils.

Once her potions were ready, she would take them into the village to sell. Coughs or colds, rheumatism, cuts and bruises, burns—it didn't matter. She knew what remedy was necessary to relieve pain, create lustrous hair, revive the impotent, whiten teeth, cure constipation, or simply heal the broken spirit. Unlike others who only pretended, she had the gift.

As she scraped pieces of root and bark, and gently picked the seeds from the plants she revered, she suddenly paused, aware of something different in the air around her—an unseen potent force. She stood up and, closing her eyes, listened quietly as she sniffed the air. There was an unfamiliar strangeness surrounding her. She felt the slight tremor of the earth and somewhere very far away, she heard the low-pitched hum.

It was a sound she knew well for it had been given to every civilization from the beginning of time. Used in all of the major religions—Hinduism, Buddhism, Jainism, Islam, Zoroastrianism and Christianity—it was the sacred universal sound. A single sustained note, a mantra, it was the melody of the angel that acted as the means of communication between the gods in the heavens and the humans on earth. It was the seraphim's song.

But something was wrong; the single note was slightly off-key. The pitch wasn't quite right. Then, because she was a *choovihni* and had the knowledge of the universe coursing through her veins, a cosmic consciousness that had been passed down to her from her mother, her grandmother, and her great grandmothers through all time, she sensed darkness and evil.

Quickly gathering her herbs, she cut her way through the field of Queen Anne's lace and yellow goldenrod, tall purple thistle and patches of red clover—the sweeter, younger sister of white clover. Normally she would have stopped along the way to smell the different scents and admire the unblemished natural beauty of nature. But she didn't stop and instead rushed toward the settlement where the *Kaulo Camio* tribe were camped on a hill.

This place had been the summer home of the gypsies for as long as there had been travelers. Once called Tusculum by the ancients, it was located in the shadows of the Villa Mondragone, so named because of the many dragons carved in its brown stone edifice. It was the place where her beautiful daughter—Carolina—had been born and then taken away by the *guardia di financa*, the Italian police. Because Carolina didn't exhibit the dark coloring of the *Kaulo Camio* tribe, it was believed that she had been stolen. Therefore she was made a ward of the Italian State and then a short time later adopted. Until only recently, Lyuba had refused to return to the place that had caused her so much pain and heartache, the place that the gypsies simply called the Old Villa.

Originally built on Roman ruins in the sixteenth century, it had survived through the centuries as home to various Catholic cardinals and periods of abandonment until most recently when it had been sold by the college of the Jesuits to the Second University of Rome. From their camp, it was an easy walk into Frascati, a rural village not yet marred by tourism.

The villagers still held on to some of the old beliefs, making it easier for the gypsies to sell their wares. But even in Frascati, there was the foul scent of change. Lyuba noticed it; the others who had been there before did as well. It was fast becoming a destination for tourists, with its fancy wine and its historical villa. Soon the *Kaulo Camio* tribe would have to find a new summer home.

Back at the camp Lyuba saw the single magpie sitting on a limb in the elm tree growing in front of her hut. It ruffled its shiny black feathers and screeched loudly; and then grew silent and watchful—a warning. When she entered her hut, she put aside the medicinals and herbs she had gathered and went to the old wooden trunk she kept near her bed.

The fragrance of frankincense, cloves, and cinnamon permeated the air when she lifted the tarnished brass latch and opened the lid. From within she carefully removed the Tarot cards and a black silk cloth. After covering the small table with the cloth, she sat, breathing in deeply the lingering scent; then she shuffled the cards, gently touching each one.

The cards themselves were well cared for but old. With great dexterity, she continued moving the cards on the silk cloth, each one covered in colorful design and detail. Then she separated the cards into the major arcane and the minor arcane.

She would begin with the simple nine-card Gypsy oracle, three rows of three. The top row—the past, the center row—the present, the bottom row—what was to come.

For a moment she only studied the cards. Then she moved her hands over them, not touching them, but feeling the zee—that primeval intelligence giving energy to all life and form. Satisfied, she picked them up and placed the cards one by one onto the black silk.

Much to her surprise, they felt warm. The reversed Justice, showing dishonesty; the High Priestess, indicating secrets not ready to be revealed; the Tower, signifying upheaval; slowly and methodically the *choovihni* searched for answers. The cards disturbed her. Each was a warning, but a warning of what Lyuba didn't yet know. She only knew that it related to the past, the present, and what was to come.

After a while, when she knew the cards would reveal no more, she sat quietly, meditating. She would wait. She would wait until the cards were ready to give her the answers she sought.

# Chapter 2

A certain peaceful but unfamiliar quietness had spread over Wood Rose Orphanage and Academy for Young Women now that Carolina Lovel and the females of intellectual genius—the F.I.G.s—Dara Roux, Mackenzie Yarborough, and Jennifer Torres—were once again all together on campus. Over the few months since Carolina had been hired to mentor them, "her girls" as Carolina thought of them, each female of intellectual genius had found the answer as to why she had been placed in Wood Rose Orphanage as an infant, or, in the case of Jennifer, as a young teenager. Having that knowledge had given their young lives a new shape and meaning. It had also given them more confidence to exist in a world where it was difficult to cope because they were so different.

They would always be considered different, or "weird," as the other resident-students at Wood Rose called them. But life itself, with its many mysteries and thorny challenges, was no longer a constant battle that had to be feared and fought. Feelings of insecurity, anger, and even guilt had been replaced by frequent periods of self-assurance and a determination to take whatever risks were necessary in order to accomplish much.

The fact that they were geniuses, and that each young woman manifested a special gift as a result of that genius, was something that would never be understood by those at Wood Rose or anywhere else because there were no explanations. But now, with the passage of time, it was more or less accepted—at least most of the time—by those who knew them.

Even more important, it was accepted by Dara, Mackenzie, and Jennifer. It was who they were and it was what defined them. Each female of intellectual genius had found the courage to acknowledge the fact that she wasn't like others, she never would be, and that was all right.

Carolina still found it hard to believe all that she and the F.I.G.s had accomplished in the short time since she had been hired by Dr. Thurgood James Harcourt, Headmaster at Wood Rose Orphanage and Academy for Young Women. Initially, it was her job to keep the F.I.G.s on a "short leash," as he impatiently explained, in order to prevent them from causing so much trouble—"expressions of creativity"—on the Wood Rose campus. Intimidated faculty members, terrified student-residents and staff, and physical damage to the campus itself were some of the minor and not-so-minor problems left in the wake of the F.I.G.s. With only a few weeks remaining before they graduated from Wood Rose, and fearing those so-called "expressions of creativity" were escalating, the headmaster had reached a point of desperation. Because of Carolina's exceptional credentials, her obvious intellect, and her pleasant personality, she was offered the position of teacher, mentor, and keeper of the F.I.G.s.

Carolina, only a little older than the F.I.G.s, gladly accepted the challenge. Having only recently learned that she was adopted, and that her adoptive parents were reaching retirement age and, therefore, no longer able or willing to finance her seemingly unending advanced educational pursuits, Carolina was looking for a change that didn't include the support of the two people she had grown up mistakenly believing to be her parents. The opportunity to work at Wood Rose and be responsible for three highly intelligent young ladies seemed perfect. She immediately moved into a small one-bedroom bungalow at the orphanage, living on the orphanage property being one of the requirements of working there.

The bonding and friendship between Carolina and the F.I.G.s, and the mutual trust, was immediate. And in just a short time, the responsibility given to Carolina to take care of and mentor these three exceptional girls provided the incentive for her to follow through with her own difficult search and to invite them to join her in that search; for Carolina had decided to find her birth parents.

It wasn't easy. All she had to guide her was a letter given to her on her eighteenth birthday, one of the conditions of her adoption. Written in an unknown language that resembled the most mysterious manuscript in the world—the Voynich Manuscript, her search took them to the small Italian village of Frascati, the place where the Voynich Manuscript was first discovered in the fifteenth century.

With help from the F.I.G.s, Carolina was able to discover the truth about her background: that her parents were gypsies from the *Kaulo Camio* tribe, and her mother was a *choovihni*—a wise woman. And even though she still had a great deal to learn, Carolina was discovering that she was also a *choovihni*, a gift she had inherited from her mother,

Lyuba, and the many generations of grandmothers before her.

Once Carolina learned why she had been given up for adoption, it was inevitable that Dara, Mackenzie, and Jennifer would want to find the answers to their own questions. Carolina, who was more like a big sister than their teacher, encouraged and supported them in finding the truth about their own birth parents. This became their mission the summer of their graduation from Wood Rose. They were a force to be recognized; they were Carolina and the three F.I.G.s.

Each female of intellectual genius had played the game: the psychic conflict between wanting primal familiarity or the search for novel experience. Familiarity was knowing and, more importantly, accepting without question who she was and her situation. The search for novel experience—knowledge of her past, however, meant uncertainty, change, leaving the bounds of familiarity for something unknown.

One was safe; the other, frightening. Yet, in the end, each F.I.G. knew what she must do. She had no choice. She wanted to learn the truth. Without that, she would never feel complete as a person. If she was to ever make sense of who she was and understand why she had been placed in an orphanage, she needed to discover the truth about her own parents. Carolina understood because she had also played the game.

Even though each journey, each search for the truth, proved overwhelmingly difficult and treacherous, Carolina and her girls pushed on, no matter the obstacles, no matter the danger—relentless and determined. Eventually, they found the answers they sought. Dara learned why her mother had abandoned her in the store when she was only five years old, Mackenzie learned why she had been placed in an orphanage right after she had been born, and Jennifer discovered the truth about why her parents faked her death as well as their own.

But now things seemed to have settled into a predictable routine on the large, sprawling Wood Rose campus dotted with massive moss-draped oak trees and beautiful elms that in the autumn of the year turned an unusual shade of orange, the color of sun-ripened apricots. An imposing stone wall surrounding the property both protected and provided privacy from the outside world for those who lived within.

Manicured walkways and flower beds filled with the colorful summer blooms of marigolds and zinnias and gladiolas, and multi-storied stone buildings housing the classrooms, dormitory, administration offices, cafeteria and library, and a small chapel named after the Alcott family who had founded Wood Rose Orphanage and Academy for Young Women, provided a safe environment for the orphans, faculty members, and staff who called Wood Rose their home.

The fear and drama—and danger—the females of intellectual genius had all experienced in their search for answers had been replaced by a serene calm. And with the end of summer approaching, the new fall term near, that calm, although somewhat unfamiliar and unnatural, had spread throughout the Wood Rose community.

Carolina was thinking of these things as she put on her makeup in her new three-bedroom bungalow with the brightly colored, hand-sewn cushions and slipcovers and pretty damask draperies she had made on the sewing machine borrowed from a neighbor, Dr. Dolores Smythe, another member of the faculty at Wood Rose. Just recently married, her one-bedroom bungalow no longer suitable, the larger home had been a gift to Carolina and her husband, Larry Gitani, when they returned from their honeymoon in Frascati, Italy, the place where Carolina had found her mother.

Carolina had met Larry at the university in Chapel Hill where they were both undergraduate students, and it was with his encouragement that she decided to suck up enough courage to search for her biological parents. Larry had provided support for her from the first day they met by giving her information that she could never have found on her own. It was Larry who was able to explain most—but not all—of the contents in the old wooden box she was given on her eighteenth birthday from her birth parents, also a condition of her adoption. It was only later that she learned that he, too, was a gypsy—the son of a gypsy king—who had chosen another life path that didn't include staying with his tribe.

Upon their return from Italy, in addition to having a new home to live in, they soon discovered there had been other changes that had taken place in their absence from Wood Rose as well.

Miss Edna Grace Alcott, the wealthy elderly niece of the founder of Wood Rose Orphanage and Academy for Young Women, and Mrs. Lilian Ball, the headmaster's long-time widowed administrative assistant, had decided to move in together and were now sharing a two-bedroom bungalow on the orphanage property not too far from Carolina and Larry. Since they were both getting up in years, or as the outspoken Miss Alcott said, "getting a little long in the tooth," it would be nice for these two long-time friends to look after one another as well as keep a sharp eye on the hard-headed, pompous, and, in their opinion, often dim-witted headmaster who was also starting to show his age—and occasional forgetfulness.

And, Jimmy Bob Doake, who with the soul of a poet for years had been the night watchman and caretaker at Wood Rose, moved from his old family home located just outside the gates of Wood Rose and down the road a bit into a single-bedroom bungalow on the orphanage property recently vacated by Mrs. Ball. This was an extraordinary accomplishment, because Jimmy Bob didn't like change. Moving from the only home he had ever known was a momentous decision for him that required a great deal of introspection and deep soul searching.

Of course, he wasn't giving up the family home, Headmaster Harcourt explained, and he could always go visit it—like a vacation home—whenever he felt the need. And since it was located only minutes from the Wood Rose gates and down the road a bit, it wouldn't be a long or tiring trip.

As further enticement, included in this arrangement

was Jimmy Bob's hound dog, Tick, who had been promoted by the headmaster to the responsible position of guard dog in order to justify having a dog living on the orphanage campus.

Tick had been the constant companion to Jimmy Bob ever since Jimmy Bob found him, abandoned, as a tiny puppy on a country dirt road. Jimmy Bob carried him home, fed him, took care of him, and most importantly, gave him love. Tick never forgot and frequently unabashedly displayed his affection and undying loyalty by giving Jimmy Bob wet, slurpy kisses accompanied by soft grunts that sounded more like a pig than a dog.

The newest members of Jimmy Bob's little family, his recently acquired cat, Carol, along with her new litter of kittens, couldn't be left out either, insisted Jimmy Bob, and the headmaster reluctantly agreed, although their justification was still to be determined.

Carol, it seems, was prolific, something brought on by occasional flights of fancy usually late at night. As a result, she had recently presented Old Tick and Jimmy Bob with four furry kittens, all black and all identical except for one spunky little female that had a white patch of fur on its forehead in the shape of a pentagram—the mark of the pentacle of Solomon. He would give that one to Carolina and Larry as a belated wedding gift as soon as she was old enough to be weaned from her fanciful mother.

Of all the changes, however, what made Carolina the happiest was something that Miss Alcott and Mrs. Ball had instigated. Because of their determination and insistence, a vacant three-bedroom bungalow had been given to the newly graduated F.I.G.s. No longer students at Wood Rose, and therefore ineligible to live in the dormitory, this would be their forever home—the place to return to—when they weren't studying at a university or travelling. Carolina saw all of these changes as positive signs and forward-moving improvements for Wood Rose.

Larry had flown out of Raleigh-Durham earlier that morning for Buenos Aires where he would be a visiting professor teaching a course in ancient Asian philosophy at the Universidad de Buenos Aires for the next six weeks. With classes not starting at Wood Rose for another two weeks when Carolina would resume her teaching obligations and the F.I.G.s would return to their university studies, Carolina and the F.I.G.s were using the free time to shop for what they would need in the weeks and months ahead.

Carolina glanced at the clock. She had told the F.I.G.s that she would pick them up at ten that morning. That way they could drive downtown for lunch at Elder's, their favorite restaurant, and have most of the afternoon free to shop. She grabbed her purse and car keys, and as she was walking to her car she felt a slight vibration. "How strange," she mumbled.

Glancing around she saw her former next-door neighbor, Dr. Dolores Smythe, expert in international affairs, geography, and politics, jogging on the walking path seemingly undisturbed. Across the way in front of the cafeteria two other faculty members, who had only recently been hired to teach science and social studies, were casually engaged in a somewhat animated conversation that involved a lot of arm flailing; and Ms. Larkins, the dorm mother, was standing outside the dormitory entrance shaking out sheets she most likely had just removed from the dryer. They also appeared not to have noticed.

Carolina had never known Raleigh to have an earthquake. In fact, the last one that was recorded had occurred in the 1930s. "How strange," Carolina repeated before climbing into her white Honda Civic.

# ChapteR 3

Dara, Mackenzie, and Jennifer loved their bungalow: deciding on color schemes, which Jennifer did because of her genius as an artist and musician; planning the placement of everything, which Mackenzie did because of her genius in math, algebra and all things pertaining to problems and space; and decorating with pieces from around the world, which Dara did because of her genius for understanding foreign, ancient, and obsolete languages. Naturally, Jennifer's paintings were the main focal point of each room in their very own, much-loved forever home.

As soon as they had moved in, once again, Carolina had borrowed Dr. Smythe's sewing machine so she could make the draperies and slipcovers with matching cushions for the F.I.G.s' new home in their choice of fabrics and colors. Frequent trips, also thanks to Carolina, were made to the local nursery so whatever was in bloom or in season could be purchased and planted in order to hopefully thrive in the small squat of the yard that was now the responsibility of the F.I.G.s.

And Miss Alcott, since the F.I.G.s were starting from scratch, and because she no longer needed all the stuff that was in her large family home now that she and Mrs. Ball lived together in a much smaller residence on the orphanage grounds, had made a determined and much concerted effort to do a good clean out of each room in the beautiful twelve-thousand-square-foot mansion located in the exclusive old-moneyed area of Raleigh's Cameron Hills with the assistance of an equally determined Mrs. Ball.

The discards included sets of dishes, silverware, furniture, carpets, pots and pans, linens—anything that the two mature and experienced women felt the F.I.G.s might need. Of course they needed everything, and the important undertaking each morning was to drive into the older upper-crust residential area of Cameron Hills after making sure Headmaster Harcourt had his mail, his coffee, his schedule for the day, and any other pointless thing he requested.

After all, the F.I.G.s were very special. With their intellectual superiority and *joie de vivre*, they had brought vim and vitality, or "piss and vinegar" as Miss Alcott called it, to a campus that would have otherwise been dull, lifeless, and boring. Even a little sad. The idea of there not being females of intellectual genius on the campus of Wood Rose Orphanage and Academy for Young Women simply didn't compute. It was their home. And now, it always would be.

As a result of all of these efforts made on their behalf, in a very short time the F.I.G.s had turned a house into a home that was uniquely theirs, rich in antique furniture, beautiful china, sterling silver pieces and place settings, Persian carpets, priceless *objets d'art* and Jennifer's paintings. They felt comfortable, settled, and secure for the first time in their young lives. Most of all, they felt extremely grateful and happy.

In a couple of weeks they would resume their formal university studies and special projects. Once back at Yale, Dara would finish her report on her discoveries of the pictographs she discovered beneath New York City's Grand Central Terminal as compared to her findings at the archaeological site in the Shandong province of China. It was a remarkable and enviable find noted throughout the world of archaeology, and her report would be published in the prestigious *Global Journal of Archaeology and Anthropology*.

Later, right after the first of the year, she would return to China, to visit another archaeological site that had recently been showing promise—this one in the Gansu province that bordered the Yellow Sea to the west and the Shandong province to the east. This was the area believed to have been first settled by gypsies near the historical village Mackenzie's mother, Ling, took them to visit when they were last there.

Then Dr. Wu would take her to see the rock paintings of Helan Mountains in northern China, and that is where their work would focus for several weeks. Thousands of petroglyphs had been discovered in that area and were believed to have been created as much as 10,000 years earlier. Dr. Wu had also mentioned another project of major interest which he wanted to discuss with Dara when he saw her.

Mackenzie would return to her lab on the campus of MIT, a laboratory set up specifically for her research on what she referred to as improving the human condition; specifically, the genetic links between humans and plants in disease prevention. Her discovery leading to finding a genetic link of immortality to the dandelion flower was already of international significance. That research would soon be advancing to the trial stage.

Then, in the new year, she would return to the Yellow Sea Laboratory in the Shandong province of China where her mother was from to continue her research for a few weeks there with other leading scientists.

*The Nightjar's Promise*, Jennifer's latest musical creation, a symphony written in C sharp major in four movements, would be performed at Carnegie Hall in New York City over Thanksgiving, along with her other original music compositions, *The Gypsy Cadence*, *The Wish Rider*, and *The Clock Flower*.

Each piece had been inspired by her best friends—Carolina, Dara, and Mackenzie. The compositions were their stories; how each had overcome tremendous heart-breaking challenges in search of information about her birth parents. The musical notes written on eight-stave paper had been given life and beauty by Jennifer's genius as a result of the pain suffered and the truth revealed. This latest composition, *The Nightjar's Promise*, was Jennifer's story.

Therefore, Jennifer would be busy with rehearsals at the famous Hall in addition to her studies at Juilliard with some of the greatest composers from around the world.

With so much going on, little thought had been given to leaving the security of Wood Rose, their new forever home, and returning to their advanced studies and overseas projects. Now, however, with only a couple of weeks left before they would be separated, the uncomfortable feeling of uncertainty and insecurity began creeping silently and pervasively into the ruffled fringe of their exciting lives. And even though they would see each other over Thanksgiving in New York City, and they were all planning to meet after the first of the year in Puli, China, near where Dara and Mackenzie would be working on their projects, the bright, exhilarating happiness they had been feeling was becoming slightly diminished.

Jennifer, being the most sensitive of the F.I.G.s, was the first to show signs of things not being quite right. Demonstrative fits of anger followed by moments of depression were displayed more often and for longer periods of time. Once again she was staying up late at night rapidly scribbling down the musical notes only she could hear onto the sheaf of eight-stave paper. She had also brought out her sketch pad and charcoals, capturing visually what she was hearing, an indication that something beyond their understanding was happening. And there was the cemetery vault—at least the memory of it, and the headstone with her parents' names on it "and daughter."

Mackenzie, either because she sensed that Jennifer was becoming more distracted and distanced, or because the insecurity she had carried with her since infancy had resurfaced, was starting to lisp again, something she hadn't done since discovering who her mother was. And she was eating more. The calculator which she had always carried with her on a belt around her waist was becoming more visible in her hands as she seemed to have more numbers to crunch, more problems to solve. Perhaps all of her questions hadn't been answered after all.

Dara was brooding a great deal and energetically applying the profanity of some ancient, foreign, or obsolete dialect more frequently to inconsequential things and matters of insignificance. The defensiveness and anger she had felt as a child was once again rising closer to the surface making it easier to vocally put on display.

There were other signs as well, signs that weren't so evident, but still felt by Dara. The painful memories of a young child being abandoned by her mother; a rusted-out trailer that was called home would suddenly be recalled without any apparent reason.

Carolina noticed the changes, even though they were subtle, because she herself was starting to feel anxious about her girls once again leaving the security of Wood Rose to lead their lives individually and separately. Even though they would talk by phone—they had all hooked up to video chat, and each had the special code word alerting the others to drop everything and meet at Carolina's bungalow because something happened that could only be dealt with by all of them, together—Carolina and the three F.I.G.s—it just wasn't the same as actually being with one another. As Carolina and the three females of intellectual genius, they were one unit; life was manageable. Separated, life was uncertain at best and at times almost impossible to navigate.

Once again difficult adjustments would have to be made.

# ChAPTER 4

"What do we want to shop for first?" The F.I.G.s and Carolina had just finished an early lunch and were driving toward the large mall in North Hills where they would most likely spend the entire day.

"I need some more digging clothes," said Dara, "since Dr. Wu has invited me to be a part of his research team again. "It will probably be pretty cold there, so I will need heavy long-sleeved shirts and a couple of warm jackets. And pockets—I want lots of pockets in my pants."

Dr. Len Wu was an expert in prehistoric, early historic, and medieval culture and cultural development in Old and New China. His work in the iconography of ancient Chinese cultures, the relationship between art and society, ancient writing systems, and Chinese historical archaeology was well known throughout the world—and to Dara. Of course, the studies he had conducted on ancient writing systems were of particular interest to her, being a female of intellectual genius with a special talent in foreign, obscure, and obsolete languages.

When Dr. Chu, Dara's faculty advisor and Dean of Language Studies at Yale, first introduced Dara to Dr. Len Wu, he had explained to Dara that in collaboration with colleagues all across China, he was undertaking investigations into early complex societies around the Neolithic site of the Longshan period dating 2500-1900 BC. His research involved work on early writing, language, and human sacrifice at the Shang Dynasty capital of Anyang and investigations of craft production and social organization during the late Neolithic and early Bronze Age in Gansu Province.

The undertaking was enormous. It was his desire that these varied investigations would allow for new views on a wide variety of topics relevant to the understanding of the Chinese civilization past and present and future. And, because of her unique understanding of languages—ancient, obsolete, and foreign, and the invaluable contributions she had already made, he was inviting Dara to once again be a part of his very elite research team of archeologists—twenty-two in all. His new focus was on the Helan Mountain rock carvings in Inner Mongolia.

"Before I go to see the Helan Mountain rock carvings, Dr. Wu wants to take me to a new site located near the Shandong and Gansu provinces, not too far from the Yellow Sea Laboratory where Mackenzie will be working." She glanced back at Jennifer sitting in the back seat with Mackenzie. "You remember, Jennifer?" trying to draw her into the conversation. "That is where Mackenzie's mother took us to see the area where it is believed gypsies once settled."

"That's right," said Mackenzie when Jennifer didn't respond. "The people who live there now have their own language and can be traced back as far as the Yuan Dynasty, sometime during the eleventh and twelfth centuries. The Chinese people called them the *Luoli*."

"Which means gypsy," Dara added. "Scholars believe that they arrived on China soil some two hundred years before moving into Europe. It might even be the place where they originated. If that is true, it will change history as it is now written."

Jennifer nodded, not really hearing what Dara or Mackenzie had said. All she could hear was the low continuous hum of B flat in the minor key—just slightly off tune. Other notes were starting to join the undertone of B flat minor, like a countermelody, with changing tempo and form.

"I need some nice slacks and blouses to wear while I am working at the Yellow Sea Laboratory. Nothing too dressy because everyone there wears white lab coats, but nicer than jeans and tee shirts. And maybe some comfortable shoes." Mackenzie moved slightly closer to Jennifer. "What about you, Jennifer? What do you want to shop for?"

The heavy rock that Jennifer always felt in her chest when something horrible was about to happen had returned. She was painfully aware of it now as she stared unseeing through the car window. She knew it was only a matter of time before black and white shapes would appear as the musical notes filled in the blank bars and measures. And then, those shapes would become images, more defined with color—recognizable; and the music would be more formed and coherent—melodious. It was something that just happened, and she couldn't stop it even if she had wanted to. She felt something, someone touching her hand. It was Mackenzie.

"What do you want to shop for?" Mackenzie repeated.

Jennifer heard her this time. The swirling black and white visions and the musical notes of mismatched sounds were fading away. She was back. She flipped her long blond ponytail. "I need some art supplies—charcoals and canvasses and more oil paints."

Carolina glanced in her rearview mirror. "We can do that," she said cheerfully. "I think I would like to find a nice men's store and get Larry a couple of dress shirts. Something he can wear when we go to New York for Jennifer's performance over Thanksgiving. Maybe I can find a new dress. Something red—or maybe black," then laughing, "or blue."

Jennifer's strange mood had passed, and for the rest of the day they were four young women enjoying each other's company and a day of shopping together. Later that evening, however, a disquieting and troubling strangeness seemed to permeate the three-bedroom bungalow that was the new home of the F.I.G.s. It was at once unexplained, yet recognizable and familiar.

They had been through this before. But before, it was because of the confusion and uncertainty they had felt brought on as they searched for their birth parents. There had also been a great deal of fear to face, even though that was harder to admit. They had been looking for answers as to why they had been abandoned—given up—placed in an orphanage. They had needed to know why they weren't wanted in order to overcome their feelings of inadequacy. They had those answers now. So why was this "thing" happening again?

As she did every night, after Mackenzie and Jennifer had already gone to their rooms, Dara checked the doors to make sure they were locked before withdrawing to her own bedroom. It was something she had always done as a very young child when it had only been her and her mother. But her thoughts weren't on door locks; rather, they were focused on an ancient language that had come to her when they were out shopping earlier in the day. It was pre-Sumerian; similar to Sanskrit and ancient Egyptian hieroglyphs, yet from an earlier time still. Maybe even before any known civilizations. It was something unfamiliar, and she couldn't find the root word of the symbols. At least nothing that was obvious.

Mackenzie had gone to her room early, and propped up with pillows in bed with her calculator that was always nearby, she was comparing various elements between music, such as its form, rhythm and meter, the pitches of its notes and the tempo of its pulse, to math as it could be related to the measurement of time and frequency. It was something she felt compelled to do in that given moment. It didn't matter that she didn't understand why.

Sitting cross-legged in the middle of her bed, pushing through the pain of the rock, Jennifer scribbled musical notes that, although far from being complete, appeared to be coming together to form a tone poem. It was a single continuous movement evoking the content of something non-musical, such as a poem, or painting, or perhaps an ancient artifact. The latter was something that had occurred to her earlier in the day while they were having lunch.

The F.I.G.s had no control over their thoughts and impulses—Dara's foreign, ancient, or obsolete languages; Mackenzie's complicated math formulations; or Jennifer's musical compositions and paintings. These instinctive, unplanned and involuntary thoughts and actions were the manifestation of what made each F.I.G. a genius. They were the coping mechanisms these females of intellectual genius had been born with and used since early childhood when they first understood that they were different.

It was also an indication that something terrible was happening over which they had no control.

Carolina got ready for bed and then turned on the television to watch the evening news while waiting for Larry to call. He had told her that he would be in a faculty meeting that evening, but would call her as soon as he got to his room.

Spending the day with her girls had been fun, although Jennifer worried her. Dara had told her that Jennifer was staying up late at night writing musical notes on her eight-stave paper, and Mackenzie had mentioned seeing some sort of charcoal drawing that Jennifer was working on as well.

Carolina had also noticed that Mackenzie was starting to lisp slightly, something she did whenever she was feeling insecure, and Dara was occasionally distracted and lost in her thoughts. And even though she didn't understand them, Carolina felt reasonably certain that the foreign words Dara was increasingly using were profanity from some ancient, foreign, or obsolete dialect. She wondered if all of this meant something they weren't aware of was about to disrupt their lives. She hoped not. They had already been through so much.

Just then there was a news alert announced on the television; something about a severe storm. Carolina turned up the volume.

*... seems to have originated as a dust storm in China... merged with another storm before moving off the African coast, and is now rapidly gaining in strength and hopscotching across the Atlantic. Early indications are that the cooler weather system moving down from Canada will prevent this category 1 hurricane named Luoli from hitting the United States and instead push it toward the north to cooler waters where it will eventually dissipate.*

*However, if it does continue on its present course, it will make it the largest hurricane in recorded history to make landfall on the east coast of the United States. Mandatory evacuations will become necessary. We will keep a watch on its progress and bring you further updates when we have them.*

# CHAPTER 5

Lyuba slept fitfully during the night, finally getting up earlier than normal to prepare for the day. She wouldn't go to the graveyard next to the creek that morning as she usually did. Instead, she went to her old wooden trunk and carefully removed the crystal globe from the folds of black silk cushioned and protected by the soft layered undercoat of llama wool. Like the Tarot cards, the crystal had been passed down to her from the generations of *choovihnis* in her family. Perhaps it could give her answers where the Tarot could not.

As she prepared the crystal on the table in front of her, outside she heard the single cry of the magpie. It was still there, sitting on the limb of the elm tree, waiting in the darkness, acknowledging her and warning her.

At first the gray swirls that appeared within the crystal were clouded, twisted and without meaning. Lyuba patiently watched, scrying she called it, her hands held slightly over the crystal, not touching yet feeling, and after a while visions appeared through the varying shades of light and dark; the meaning became clear.

She understood the reason for the vibration of earth's energies she felt the day before, the scent of places far beyond earth and distant to all that was familiar, and the seraphim's song. She knew there was danger so great that the survival of everything known to man and humanity itself was being threatened.

For some unknown reason this danger was directed toward her daughter and the three girls. And lurking in the shadows, hiding, was a perfidious evil that went by the name of Milosh. These were the answers the crystal imparted to her because as a true *choovihni* only she could understand.

She took several deep breaths and closed her eyes. She could see her daughter, Carolina, and feel her concern for the three young women she cared about, Dara, Mackenzie, and Jennifer. As the early morning sun gently rose over the horizon, the black magpie sat silently, watching, listening, while somewhere nearby an owl hooted. Another warning.

Over and over again, Lyuba repeated the words in her mind, and then whispered them, willing them to be heard and understood by her precious daughter. But she couldn't get through. Something was preventing her words of warning from reaching her daughter, Carolina.

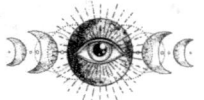

It was the middle of the night when the energetic eighty-seven-year-old Miss Alcott awoke with a start. By "middle of the night," it was not quite ten o'clock, still hours before what Jimmy Bob poetically referred to as the "witches' moments"—the magical time that occurs between late darkness and early light.

With the new project taking precedence over everything else, all of the cleaning out and sorting through things in Miss Alcott's large stately home and moving them into the little home now belonging to the F.I.G.s at Wood Rose, the two new roommates—Miss Edna Grace Alcott and Mrs. Lilian Ball—were finding it increasingly difficult to stay awake in the evenings.

Before, when there had been no project to occupy them, the time after supper had been spent in stimulating conversation, recalling happy and some not-so-happy memories from their childhoods, usually resulting in a bad case of the silly giggles, before retiring to their separate bedrooms at the established ten o'clock bedtime. Lately, however, it had now become a quiet time—a time for contemplation and relaxation—a time for nodding off.

The whole ordeal of driving into Raleigh in early-morning traffic after getting Thurgood squared away, and then spending most of the day packing things into boxes to give to the females of intellectual genius was exhausting. Not to mention the furniture that required a great deal more effort, thought, and planning. For that involved Jimmy Bob and his truck and usually a couple of additional able-bodied men with strong backs. The enthusiasm and willingness were still there, but the roommates weren't as young as they once were and, therefore, the bodies not as able. To compensate, the ten o'clock bedtime hour had now been revised to the much earlier hour of seven o'clock.

Therefore, when Edna Grace awoke a few minutes before the original bedtime hour of ten o'clock, fully rested, filled with a feeling of *esprit de corps*, and ready to charge forth and seize the day, it was interesting, if not downright curious. She immediately padded barefooted into Lilian's bedroom. "Wake up, Lilian, I've just remembered something else."

Lilian was used to Edna Grace "remembering something else" at all hours of the day and night, so she wasn't startled when she felt Edna Grace gently shaking her. In fact, it reminded her of her late husband and how he would also remember something else, usually in the middle of the night.

"There is a big closet—a safe room actually—where I stored my most precious valuables. Under the stairs. We need to get those things out so I can give them to Carolina for her to keep. I want her to have them."

"That's nice," Lilian responded, her eyes barely open. "We will do that in the morning." She reached for the blanket to pull it more securely around her shoulders.

"We need to go now," insisted Edna Grace wringing her hands. "This is important." Sensing that Lilian wasn't exactly eager, she added what she hoped would be an enticement, "And we will avoid that horrible early-morning rush-hour traffic."

It was the way she stressed the word "important," however, that got Lilian's attention. She raised up leaning on her elbow and looked closely at her friend. She wasn't walking in her sleep, as she had done on a few occasions since moving into their new home at Wood Rose, she certainly seemed alert and focused, and she was obviously determined to go to the mansion right then. Lilian knew from experience it wouldn't do any good to try to talk her out of it. She sighed, yawned, threw back the covers and began dressing.

Within the hour Edna Grace and Lilian were pulling out boxes of family heirlooms, velvet cases filled with valuable jewelry, old albums stuffed with photographs that had been meticulously identified with purple ink, and sealed boxes that had the word *PRECIOUS* written on the outside also in purple ink. They didn't bother to open those; they simply carried them outside and shoved them into the trunk of Lilian's car to be taken to Carolina.

Fortunately, the safe room, hidden under a long flight of steep stairs, was large, somewhat ventilated—although musty smelling from being closed up, and had been wired for electricity. The concealed door leading to and from the safe room, however, was rather small, making it necessary for them to scrunch down and bend over every time they needed to remove a box of something valuable and irreplaceable from the room any way that they could. This usually involved kicking it, scooting it, and manhandling it until it was then packed into the car.

When they returned to Wood Rose, the sun was up and bright, and breakfast was already being served in the cafeteria to the student-residents, faculty and staff. Rather than taking the time to change clothes and eat breakfast, however, both women went directly to Lilian's office so they could relax their stiff cramped muscles and sore swollen feet with a much-needed nice cup of tea before sorting the mail, preparing the day's schedule for Headmaster Harcourt, and putting into motion whatever else was needed for Wood Rose to get the day started. It was while they sipped their tea that the heady decision was made to unload the car at Carolina's bungalow sometime after lunch—or, perhaps, right before dinner.

When the headmaster arrived a short time later, oddly and most noticeably, his normally punctual administrative assistant Mrs. Ball was not at her desk, and Miss Alcott, who since moving onto the Wood Rose campus was usually loitering around nearby, seemed to be missing in action as well. When he opened the door to his office, he was startled to find the two elderly women stretched out on the soft, overstuffed green velvet sofa, their shoes neatly lined up on the thick-piled oriental carpet, and two empty tea cups placed in saucers on the nearby table in his beautiful, dark mahogany-paneled office. Both were sound asleep.

# CHAPTER 6

Larry had been checking his phone and getting regular updates on the storm whose mass already surpassed any other hurricane in recorded history including two which were considered the largest—the Great Galveston Hurricane of 1900 when between 6,000 and 8,000 people died, and the 1928 Okeechobee Hurricane, also known as the Hurricane San Felipe Segundo, when up to 4,000 people died.

Indications showed it rapidly moving toward the east coast of the United States, and its path through the warm tropical waters of the Gulf Stream had caused it to gain strength. It was now a category 3, and if it kept on the projected course, it would make landfall somewhere near the North Carolina Outer Banks later that evening. The National Weather Service was predicting that by then it would be upgraded to a category 5.

He had tried calling Carolina that morning before going to his class, but she apparently had already left the bungalow and forgotten to take her phone with her, or the battery on the phone was dead. She was always forgetting to plug it in so it would recharge.

When they had talked the night before, she mentioned planning to take the F.I.G.s out for breakfast. He would try to reach her between classes. More than likely she was tracking the storm, but it had developed so quickly and he would just feel better if he knew for sure. Everyone at Wood Rose would need to start making preparations. This would be a bad one simply because of its mammoth size. The damage would be catastrophic; and the potential death toll enormous.

When the sun was positioned directly overhead, and the elm tree and its shadow had become one, Lyuba knew she could wait no longer. All of her efforts to reach Carolina had been obstructed. Whatever the force was, it was too great, even for a *choovihni*. Something was interfering with the natural order of all things animate and inanimate, corporal and spiritual in this world and beyond. She didn't know what it was other than it was completely out of control. The destruction this could cause was unimaginable, and somehow Carolina and the F.I.G.s were involved.

She opened the top drawer of the old burled maple armoire where she kept important things and removed a small piece of paper wrapped in a scrap of lace. She reached into her pocket and felt for her talisman—the small rock with a natural hole. Carefully tucking the paper next to it within the folds of her skirt, she hurried from her hut and through the field toward the farm and vineyard. It was a place she knew well.

It was the home where the signor and signora lived. Settlers. Mother Granchelli and Papa, they insisted on being called. It was where Carolina and the F.I.G.s had stayed when they visited Frascati before, and more recently, where her daughter and new husband stayed for their honeymoon. Even though they were settlers and unfamiliar with the ways of the travelers, Lyuba knew the Granchellis could be trusted. They would help her if they could.

When she approached the old farm house, the large heavily carved wooden front door opened and Signora Granchelli rushed out, her arms spread wide to embrace this gypsy woman who because of Carolina and the F.I.G.s had become like family. She knew Lyuba would come. "The storm!" she exclaimed. "Do they know?"

She didn't need to explain who "they" were or what she meant. Lyuba knew things the Italian mother would never know or understand, but Mother Granchelli knew enough, and her fear was real and warranted.

Lyuba reached into her pocket and pulled out the slip of paper to give to her. It had a number written in pencil on it. It was the number she had called in desperation one time before when she knew Carolina and the girls were in danger and she couldn't contact them to give warning. Somehow, calling that number had reached a woman who also shared her concern—and love—for her daughter and her daughter's young friends. She had helped. Lyuba prayed that she would be able to help again.

# CHAPTER 7

Not wanting to disturb the slumbering women, Headmaster Harcourt went back into Mrs. Ball's office where he sorted through his own mail, and then tried to fix a cup of coffee that tasted more like water a dirty dishrag had been soaked in. Unhappy with the results of trying to fix a cup of coffee, and bothered by the fact that two old women sleeping on his sofa in his office just didn't look very professional, what had started out as a relatively nice, pleasant day was quickly becoming bleak and not very promising.

To make matters worse, his wife had been gone for a week, the first of a three-week visit with her aging mother who lived in a retirement home in the city of Charlotte, about 165 miles away near the South Carolina border.

At first he had looked forward to having the time alone; being free to eat what he wanted, stay up as late as he wanted, watch his favorite shows on television, and just being on his own. He had even considered pulling out all of those boxes from the hall closet where he had stored the parts and miles of track for an N gauge model train set he was planning to set up one day, probably after he retired. Maybe he would start work on putting that together in the evenings just for fun.

But after a week, he was tired of bologna sandwiches and watching worthless, brain-numbing television shows.

And all of the boxes with model train parts and miles of track were still crammed in the closet and untouched. Plus, he missed his wife.

Just then the telephone rang. Unfamiliar with the complicated and what he believed to be byzantine phone system on Mrs. Ball's desk, with the flashing red lights that demanded some sort of urgent action, numerous blinking yellow buttons that were supposed to connect to important people when pushed, and an intimidating large black knob that he suspected could reach beyond outer space, he simply sat back and stared at the noisy contraption.

Startled awake by the ringing, Mrs. Ball immediately jumped up from the sofa, smoothed the wrinkles on her blouse and skirt, and rushed over to the headmaster's desk to answer the phone. A voice speaking in broken English— an Italian accent she guessed—told her to please wait. Then a second voice, this one vaguely familiar, began to speak in the soft heavily accented tones she recognized from another phone call she had received—not so long ago. Without being told, she knew it was Carolina's mother. It was Lyuba.

Frantically she motioned to Miss Alcott who had also been awakened by the urgent, irritating sound of the phone. With her friend now listening on the phone with her, they heard Lyuba tell them that her daughter and the three young girls she loved were in terrible danger. This woman from another time, another place, maybe even another universe for all they knew, had reached out to Mrs. Ball once before because of tremendous need. She was reaching out again, and there was no doubt or hesitation that they would do everything in their power to help her.

She needed to get a message to her daughter—please—they heard Lyuba say.

"They must seek safe shelter. When the leaves turn away from the heavens to face the earth, they must hide. You must hide. Everyone is in danger. When the seraphim sings, a key will be given to her. She needs to listen for the seraphim's song. She needs to watch for the key and protect it from evil. She must return it to where it belongs."

Both women began talking to the gypsy woman at once. "We will find Carolina immediately and give her your message," Mrs. Ball said with authority. "What danger?" asked Miss Alcott. "What does the key look like?" asked Mrs. Ball. "What's a seraphim?" asked Miss Alcott. But the phone went dead. The message had been sent; it had been received.

Not wasting any time, Mrs. Ball and Miss Alcott put on their shoes and rushed out of the headmaster's office, past the confused, gaping-mouthed headmaster, and out of the administration building toward the three-bedroom bungalow where Carolina and Larry now lived. Finding no one at home, they hurried over to a single-bedroom bungalow, stepped over the large guard dog that was sleeping on the porch, and banged loudly on the front door. At that moment Jimmy Bob was channeling his poetic instincts from his literary muse and composing a new free verse poem when the front door suddenly burst open.

"You need to let us know just as soon as Carolina returns," ordered Mrs. Ball.

"This is extremely urgent," said Miss Alcott, and

then added, "It might be a matter of life or death."

Jimmy Bob might have had the gentle soul of a poet, but he also had the heart of a warrior when it came to fulfilling his duties as caretaker and night watchman for Wood Rose Orphanage and Academy for Young Women—especially when it came to Ms. Lovel. Unlike the other professors at Wood Rose who occasionally teased him about his passion for writing poetry, she was the one person who understood and encouraged his interest, and had even given him a book that explained the different types of poems.

He had waved to her and those three young women called F.I.G.s on their way out earlier that morning thinking they were probably going out for breakfast. He and his trusty, watchful hound dog would go wait by the front gate for them to return so he could tell Ms. Lovel that Mrs. Ball and Miss Alcott needed to see her urgently.

Everyone on campus called Carolina by her given name and had from the day she arrived because that was what she preferred. However, it had almost caused a scandal when the three F.I.G.s—her students—called her by her first name.

From the very beginning when Wood Rose first opened its doors, the faculty had always been called "Professor so-and-so" or "Dr. so and so," and the staff had always been called "Mr." or "Mrs." or "Miss" or even "Ms. so-and-so," but never by the first name. That was the tradition, and that was the rule. But over time, this behavior of calling Carolina by her first name that had been considered an act of rude irreverence and downright disrespect by other members of the faculty and staff, and especially Dr. Harcourt, became something tolerated and familiar. As a result, everyone called her Carolina.

Except for Jimmy Bob.

To Jimmy Bob, she was Ms. Lovel, and even though she was now married, she had decided to keep her maiden name. Therefore, she was and would always be—at least to Jimmy Bob—Ms. Lovel.

Not being able to talk to Carolina directly right then, and feeling they had let Lyuba down somehow but not knowing what else they could do, Mrs. Ball and Miss Alcott went home so they could freshen up and prepare for whatever unknown danger was heading their way.

Back at the old rambling farm house just on the outskirts of the small village of Frascati, Italy, the phone call accomplished, Lyuba needed still more assistance from Mother Granchelli, but she was reluctant to ask. She wasn't sure the settler would understand or would even want to help her. It was also risky to involve a settler in the practices of travelers.

Mother Granchelli was quick to admit to Lyuba she wouldn't understand anything until she had her usual mid-morning cup of espresso coffee. Especially since she hadn't slept well the night before worrying about Carolina and those three young ladies who were like her own children.

Sitting across the kitchen table from one another, drinking coffee and eating a slice of bread Mother Granchelli had baked fresh that morning, with homemade jelly made from the Granchelli vineyard grapes, Lyuba finally was able in simple terms to make the settler understand—at least partially—what she needed.

Lyuba would return to the graveyard near the creek, and her friend, Mother Granchelli, would go with her. There the two women would chant and make an offering and ask the forces of good to protect Carolina and all those she embraced from the forces of evil.

Mother Granchelli agreed without hesitation. She didn't need to know why or understand how it worked; only that the gypsy wanted her positive vibes, as a woman who loved Carolina and the F.I.G.s, to join her own positive vibes in saying the words and making the offering that would thwart the evil. Together, these two strong women—a traveler and a settler—could accomplish what was needed. At least that is what they hoped.

With much to do and no time to waste, Lyuba and Mother Granchelli set out across the field of Queen Anne's lace, yellow goldenrod, purple thistles, and patches of red clover toward the old graveyard near the creek. As they hurried, the urgency of what they intended to accomplish seemed to be magnified by warnings all around them. The earth trembled ominously beneath their feet; the hum was loud, insistent and upsetting; their skirts billowed in the strong gusting wind; and the feeling that something terrible and unexplained was happening caused them great anxiety.

But they were undeterred. Their mission was critical; it was necessary; and they would not stop until it, like the phone call, had been accomplished.

# CHAPTER 8

Those already at the dig site noticed immediately. This sullen gypsy Dr. Stanwick had hired was never in a good mood, but there were times when his mood was so dark and menacing, that no one wanted to be around him. So when he showed up at the site late that morning, not greeting anyone, shoulders slumped, with a scowl on his face, they knew to leave him alone as they watched him shuffle over to an area to dig that was far removed from everyone else. Even Dr. Stanwick, who normally paid close attention to what Milosh was doing, felt it best to stay away from the angry young man.

At some point during the day, the others noticed that Milosh wasn't around. He had probably gone back to his trailer, they surmised. The mood around the camp immediately grew lighter. Conversations were more cheerful. Laughter and optimism filled the air about their task at hand and all they were accomplishing.

But then sometime later they saw him working near the entrance to the cave in the direct sun, and they wondered where he had been. Some even wondered if he had actually gone into the cave. Maybe he didn't know about the pig dragon.

They continued to keep their distance, preferring to

leave him alone.

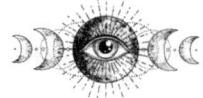

Jimmy Bob and Tick had been waiting for several hours outside the large, ornamental black wrought iron gates leading onto the Wood Rose property when at last he recognized Ms. Lovel's white Honda Civic approaching. He quickly got out of his truck and waved for her to stop.

"Mrs. Ball and Miss Alcott need to see you as soon as possible, Ms. Lovel," he said without any of the usual friendly preliminary greetings and small talk. Wanting to be as accurate as possible with the words he had been charged with, he added, "It might be a matter of life or death." He opened the gates then so the four young women could drive through.

As soon as the gates opened, a sharp pain from the heavy rock that Jennifer had carried in her chest since childhood took her breath away, and the image of a violent storm formed in Jennifer's mind. The gray, nondescript swirls she had been seeing and had captured on canvas board with charcoal were better defined now. Yellow was a new prominent color—brassy in hue. It was some sort of cylindrical object surrounded by dark black, gray, and purple clouds. Jennifer bent over in pain as the sound of the single, low octave musical note in B flat minor blocked out all other sounds around her.

The images and the musical notes that filled Jennifer's every thought, every cell in her body, and penetrated her very soul always came unexpectedly. Eventually she would be able to structure the images into a painting, and capture the random notes into a coherent musical composition. It was what made her a genius.

"My gosh! What…" Mackenzie looked back at Jimmy Bob, then at Dara and Jennifer and Carolina. Fearful that something terrible and unknown was about to happen, she didn't try to say anything else because she knew she wouldn't be able to get the words out without lisping. Instead, she turned her thoughts to the ancient Chinese mathematical principles of sound. Silently, she stared straight ahead as she envisioned expressions of musical scales in terms of numerical ratios, and in particular, the ratios of small integers.

Numbers. They had always been her friends. Numbers were what she turned to when she became afraid. Or when she felt insecure. They were what made her a genius.

Dara remained stoic as her thoughts turned toward symbols that she imagined had come from another world, another galaxy. The mental exercise she always did whenever familiarizing herself with a new language was her private world—her private language; it was how her mind functioned. It was what made her a genius.

By establishing the root of each main word, or symbol in some cases, and then assigning it a certain "weight" or number, she could figure out the origin of the word. From that, it was just a short step to recognizing its meaning.

It was her own system, something she had taught herself as a child. It worked, it had always worked, whether she was learning a new alphabet, the characters from an obsolete Chinese dialect, or hieroglyphics. But why was she thinking of this now?

As she focused on trying to find the root of the symbols in her thoughts, something from her childhood flashed through her mind. The memory of croaking tree frogs and cicadas, sitting on the concrete porch steps next to the woman with bright red lipstick, and ditch water tickling her feet. *You wait right here, pretty girl. I'll be back...*

"They are at their bungalow," Jimmy Bob told Carolina as she passed through the gates.

"Thank you, Jimmy Bob." Then for Tick's benefit, "Such a good dog." Forgetting the bags of groceries in the trunk they had shopped for on their way home, Carolina drove directly to the neat, well-kept bungalow where Mrs. Ball and Miss Alcott lived. Worried that one of the elderly women might be ill, Carolina, Dara, Mackenzie, and Jennifer didn't notice the thick darkening, threatening clouds overhead, or the large swollen drops of rain, or the strong swirling gusts of wind that turned and twisted the leaves on the trees away from the heavens to look down toward the earth. They knocked on the door, and it was immediately opened by Mrs. Ball to let them in.

With both Mrs. Ball and Miss Alcott trying to deliver the urgent message they had received from Carolina's mother at the same time, exactly as they had received it, but not quite succeeding, it was difficult at first to comprehend what they were saying. But finally Carolina managed to figure it out. She understood.

It was then that she heard Lyuba's voice—her mother's voice. *Danger is heading your way, precious daughter. Be careful.* Ever since finding her mother in that gypsy camp in Frascati, Italy, she had been hearing her mother's warnings whenever danger was near. Never in complete conversations, but words or phrases, brief sentences, and an intangible telepathic understanding.

It was unsettling, but yet those warnings had saved her life when the gypsy boy cursed her; they had saved Dara from that horrible mob beneath Grand Central Terminal where she searched for her mother; they had saved Mackenzie from the poisonous milk witch in China when she learned who her mother was; and they had saved Jennifer from the evil group of Nazis—the Fourth Reich.

Lyuba was a *choovihni*, and as the daughter of a *choovihni*, Carolina had inherited certain gifts. Communicating with her mother telepathically was one of those gifts that she was only just starting to realize. And she knew she must take the warning seriously.

She didn't understand what the danger was; only that it was imminent. Lyuba wouldn't have gone to all the trouble to get the message to her unless it was critical. And for whatever reason, she was having trouble making Carolina hear her warning. Mother Granchelli must have helped her make the phone call, she reasoned, because the *Kaulo Camio* tribe didn't use phones. She would try to figure out what the danger was and worry about the meaning of the key and the seraphim later.

"It must be that storm," said Carolina. "It must have

turned and is now heading toward the east coast."

Dara pulled up the weather map on her phone. "The storm has changed course. It is heading toward the Outer Banks." And then an expletive, "*Shekoo, baboo!*"

Lyuba said they must hide. When Carolina had first been hired at Wood Rose, the headmaster had told her about a large safe area in the basement of the dormitory that had been fixed up in the event of severe weather, a plague of locusts, a nuclear blast, or some other dire impending threat. Ms. Larkins, as dorm mother, was responsible for it. Not knowing for certain what the threat was or how long it would be a threat, she only hoped Ms. Larkins had kept it supplied.

It didn't take long for the women to formulate a plan. Mrs. Ball and Miss Alcott would inform the headmaster that danger was approaching and everyone needed to take shelter in the basement of the dormitory immediately. In the event they weren't stored or backed up elsewhere, either on a cloud or otherwise, he and the two women would have to secure all of his computer files, discs, important documents and records, and take everything with them to the basement. "Be sure to get any insurance papers as well," Carolina reminded Mrs. Ball.

The F.I.G.s would notify all of the faculty and staff to stop whatever they were doing and immediately relocate to the safe area. Thinking ahead, "Mackenzie, call your mother and let her know what we are doing. Otherwise she will be worried," said Carolina. Mackenzie had only recently learned that her biological mother was a U.S. Senator, Senator Xing-Ling Yi from Hawaii. "Jennifer, you should call Steven Schomer. He will be able to get a message to your parents." Steven Schomer was the lawyer who handled all of Jennifer's family's affairs. He had been responsible for staging the deaths of her parents as well as her own. He would know where they were and be able to contact them.

Carolina would get Jimmy Bob to help her and Ms. Larkins to move all of the student-residents—the orphans—to the basement. He would also have to make sure the generator was operable in case they lost electricity, assuming they even had a generator. She didn't remember seeing one. And she would call Larry.

When they went outside to perform their urgent tasks, a sudden force of sustained wind blew against the door. Fortunately, with Dara's help, Miss Alcott was able to shut it before it was ripped off the hinges, but it bruised her arm and it frightened the women, causing them to feel completely vulnerable, making the seriousness of the situation real and their urgent tasks even more so.

Concerned that Ms. Lovel might need something after hearing whatever it was that Miss Alcott and Mrs. Ball wanted to talk to her about that was so important, Jimmy Bob had left his post at the front gate and disregarded his usual routine of driving around the inside perimeter of the orphanage campus to make sure everything was secure and as it should be. Instead, he parked in front of Miss Alcott's and Mrs. Ball's two-bedroom bungalow watching and waiting—just to be there if needed. When all of the women suddenly rushed outside at once, and seeing the door almost get blown away, he knew that he was needed.

# ChAPTER 9

Without Mrs. Ball there to tell him, Headmaster Harcourt wasn't sure what was on his schedule for the day. As he waited for his much experienced and highly qualified administrative assistant to return after her quick departure and tell him, he turned on the small television in his office. There was some sort of severe weather alert. He knew there was a storm out in the Atlantic, but the last time he had checked, a cool front moving down from Canada together with a warm front moving up from Mexico was going to push it back out to sea before it could reach the east coast.

He moved closer to look at the map being displayed in great detail and full color on the television screen. Positioned just off the Outer Banks, there was a prominent mark with the number 5 in its center, indicating a category 5 hurricane. All of the directional lines that had previously shown the storm moving back out into the Atlantic now merged into one fat line, and that line appeared to be pointing directly at Wood Rose Orphanage and Academy for Young Women in Raleigh, North Carolina. Surely there was some mistake, but when Mrs. Ball and Miss Alcott rushed into his office without even knocking and started giving him orders, he knew there was no mistake.

It took a bit of doing to get everyone notified and

then convinced to move to the basement of the dormitory. Most hadn't heard anything about the storm, while others had assumed, as Dr. Harcourt did, that it would get pushed back out into the Atlantic Ocean. Several on the staff didn't even know about the safe room. All of this required brief, unsatisfying, and time-wasting explanations.

One member of the faculty complained that his freedom of religion, given that the hurricane was an act of nature and, by extension, the gods, was very close to being severely tampered with when he was told he *must* evacuate to the dormitory basement by three strange young women who were known on the campus as the F.I.G.s. And, even more adamant, Dr. George Connoly, professor of physics and chemistry, felt his rights as an academic with two post-graduate degrees were being infringed upon. Both men got into a rather heated argument on their way to the basement over predestination and free will.

There were some who felt they had plenty of time to pack things that were irreplaceable to take with them to the secure place where they would wait out a storm that most likely would never even get there. After all, Raleigh was in-land, not on the coast.

Dr. Dolores Smythe, professor of international affairs, geography, and politics, and Carolina's former next door neighbor, decided it was the perfect time to go through several shoe boxes of old photographs she had shoved under her bed and sort them into two piles. One pile she would take with her to the safe room; the other pile she would leave behind. She felt the whole thing was probably some sort of hoax anyway to get higher television ratings since the weather people seemed to be having such a hard time figuring out the path of the storm—if there even was a storm.

Dr. Catherine Sullivan, head of the history department, who dabbled in astrology, confided in her friend, Professor Clyde Benson, who was head of the physical education department, that she thought it might be some sort of government cover-up. Then she whispered, much to his amusement, "I think that the aliens—the Greys—are on their way." As though to prove her point, she felt it necessary to explain everything she knew about these extraterrestrials. "They are also called Zeta Reticulans, and they abduct people. They have big heads and wrap-around eyes, and some have four webbed fingers and feet, while others only have three." Then she whispered, "All of their organs are internal." She raised her eyebrows to accentuate that last statement.

And there were the two professors who had been recently hired to teach in the areas of science and social studies. They didn't know Carolina or the three so-called females of intellectual genius that well and, therefore, resented that because of them, they were being told what to do. When Miss Alcott overheard them complaining, she made it her task to convince them in no uncertain and rather unladylike terms to move their butts to the safe room immediately if they wanted to keep their teaching jobs and the perks that went along with those jobs.

Once moved to the safe area, the younger female residents were frightened by the howling wind and the sudden loud noises of things breaking and crashing outside. But it wasn't just because of the storm that they were frightened, they didn't like being in a spooky basement either. And not only that, it smelled funny. Several of them had started to whimper and were on the verge of crying, but with the help of her assistants, Ms. Larkins was able to resolve the stressful issue with small cups of ice cream. Fortunately, there were no orphaned infants at Wood Rose and hadn't been for well over a year. If there had been babies, it would have created even more problems, logistical and otherwise.

The older female student-residents seemed to revel in the fact that their normally dull and unimaginative routine had been replaced by something different and exciting. Feeling empowered and mature beyond their years, they took on the responsibility of looking after and comforting the younger girls, some with more success than others.

Lynda—spelled with a "y"—who would be graduating the next term and who had always appreciated and even admired the creative expressions of the F.I.G.s while they had been students at Wood Rose, comfortably positioned herself on a large floor cushion in one corner of the room where she began to tell stories to anyone who wanted to listen.

They were stories that sounded somewhat familiar, which they were, because they were about all of the creative expressions the F.I.G.s had accomplished over the years, usually in the darkness of night and quite often destructive, while being student-residents at Wood Rose. The severe pruning of Dr. Harcourt's prized red-tipped bush—his *Photinia frasen*—into a phallic symbol and the aluminum foiling of everything in his office, gorilla glue in the door locks and the removal of all the lightbulbs in the administration offices. And who could forget those infamous pornographic magazines? And then, of course, what they did to poor old Tick in the Alcott Chapel—just to mention a few. Lynda remembered everything—in rich detail—and those who wanted to listen included just about everyone. Except for Carolina and the F.I.G.s, of course.

By nightfall, everyone who was known to have been a member of the Wood Rose community was now settled in the well-organized basement. Ms. Larkins, with Jimmy Bob's help, had set up cots for all of the student-residents in one area, along with board games, decks of cards, and a small television. Other cots for the adults were located across the room along with tables and chairs. A long table had also been set up against one wall with snacks, a large urn of coffee, bottles of water and juice, and other things that might be desired to satisfy hunger and thirst.

At the far end of the large area, away from all of the activity, was a large wire kennel with a litter box on one end, neatly stacked cans of cat food, and a big fluffy pillow. A blue towel was loosely draped over the outside to provide privacy for Carol and her litter of four young kittens who were sleeping comfortably and to help keep them from feeling anxious.

Over the years old furniture that had been switched out for new in the administration offices and elsewhere on campus had been stored in the basement. Miss Alcott and Mrs. Ball soon commandeered two stuffed recliners and rested comfortably near the table that held all of the snacks and drinks. Headmaster Harcourt sat on one of the cots, flanked by cardboard boxes filled with irreplaceable files, computer discs, and important papers, watching everyone else.

Several of the professors had brought their laptop computers so that they could monitor the storm, at least until their batteries went dead. Others searched on their phones trying to get updates whenever they could get access.

Before leaving her bungalow, Dr. Smythe, after trying to sort through one shoe box of old photos, had given up. She didn't even recognize most of the people in the photos, so the effort of trying to preserve them seemed unproductive to say the least. She elected instead to bring a book to read, resolving to pitch all of the photos into the trash once the storm had passed.

Everything appeared to be well organized, in place, and functional initially. However, because everyone was feeling anxious, unintentional movements and subconscious actions had caused cots, tables, and chairs to be inadvertently and sometimes deliberately moved around. What had been organized soon looked disorganized.

Sometime during the night, after a particularly loud crashing noise, Carolina ventured upstairs to the main floor to peer out of a window. It was too dark to see anything, but as she went back down the stairs, looking out over the safe room and everyone there, Carolina couldn't help but notice that the position of everything—the cots, tables, chairs, and even people—now, interestingly enough, seemed to replicate the Canis Major constellation, home of the Sirius or

Dog Star, the brightest star in the night sky heavens.

With everything taken care of at Wood Rose, Jimmy Bob had gone out earlier to make sure anything loose that could be a projectile was secured. Then he drove over to his family home just down the road beyond the gates of Wood Rose to see what needed to be done there. Once there, though, with the pounding rain and the fury of wind already uprooting some of the smaller trees, he realized it was too dangerous and there was little he could do other than get soaked from the torrential rain. Therefore, he decided to return to the dry, safe area at Wood Rose. When he got back to his truck, however, Tick was gone.

Frantic, Jimmy Bob called and whistled for his dog in the increasingly treacherous storm, but Tick didn't come. He tried to drive around, looking for his trustworthy pet, but it was simply too hazardous and too dark to see. With no other choice, he slowly made his way in the darkness through the heavy rain squalls, strong wind gusts, falling tree limbs, and downed power lines back to Wood Rose.

Carolina's heart broke when Jimmy Bob told her that his faithful companion was lost in the storm. Drenched from the rain, Carolina got him a towel and a bottle of water. "Tick probably found a safe place to stay until the storm passes," she said, trying to comfort this sensitive man with the soul of a poet. "He is such a smart dog, Jimmy Bob. His instincts must have led him to a nice dry place where he will be out of the storm." She patted his hand. "If he doesn't come back on his own, the F.I.G.s and I will help you search for him just as soon as the storm passes."

But Jimmy Bob was inconsolable. Tick was gone, and it was his fault for taking him out in the storm. He moved over to the kennel against the wall where he had placed it earlier and sat on the floor next to it so he could at least take care of the other furry members of his little family.

Several times during the night the electricity flickered and went out. Thanks to Jimmy Bob, the generator kicked in so that the safe room wasn't put in total darkness. It was during those times when the generator was running that Carolina heard her mother's voice. It was fragmented and difficult to understand, but the words she did understand had to do with a key and finding a safe place for it. *Watch for the key, my daughter.* The last word she heard before the generator stopped was something that frightened her, however. Maybe she had misunderstood, but with the instincts of the daughter of a *choovihni*, she knew she hadn't misunderstood.

"What was the word, Carolina?" Dara looked up from the long list of abstract symbols she had been working with. The four young women had set up an area that was away from everyone else and private—at least as private as they could be considering everything. They each had with them their backpacks, all matching, a gift from Carolina when they went to Frascati, Italy.

Jennifer hadn't stopped writing musical notes, phrases, and measures on her eight-stave paper since getting to the safe room. Mackenzie was concentrating on her calculator where she had entered numerous difficult calculus equations and algorithms and something she called a whisker plot chart.

"Milosh."

Jennifer looked up from the musical composition she was writing, and Mackenzie stopped fingering in the difficult calculations.

"Lyuba said 'Milosh?' That horrible gypsy guy who had such a bad attitude?" Dara glanced at the other F.I.G.s.

"He tried to kill you," Mackenzie whispered, stumbling on the word 'kill.'

Carolina nodded. She wasn't wrong. Her mother was trying to warn her about the young gypsy who had put a curse on her when she and the F.I.G.s had gone to Frascati, Italy, to find out who her biological mother and father were.

# Chapter 10

At the old graveyard next to the ancient tree with low spreading limbs that had survived centuries of storms, droughts, disease, and battles between men, Mother Granchelli silently and respectfully watched Lyuba make her preparations. It was a chant that had been used by the *choovihni* for as long as there had been gypsies—since the beginning of time. It was the same chant that this *choovihni* had used once before to save her daughter, when her daughter's young man, the son of a gypsy king, helped her.

Nearby, an owl hooted—again, a warning. This time more urgent. Soon there would be no time left.

First Lyuba handed her friend the clean sheet of paper. Mother Granchelli wrote on it a blessing for Carolina, as Lyuba instructed her, and then a wish to protect her. Lyuba wrapped the paper around the small stone that had always been with her; her good luck charm. The talisman she always kept with her. Kneeling by the tree she scattered bread and wine, and, finally, water from the nearby creek.

"Tree mother, I feed you; feed me in return." She recited the spell, and, holding her friend's hand, Mother Granchelli repeated it. "Tree mother, I quench your thirst; quench mine in return." Again her friend repeated the words. When she finished, Lyuba buried the paper at the base of the tree, saying, finally, "Tree mother, I bring you a gift; bless me in return." Lyuba and Mother Granchelli put their hands on the trunk of the tree, then, wrapping their arms around the old trunk, they chanted, "Rain falls, wind blows, sun shines, grass grows." They repeated it three times before walking away without looking back.

Lyuba returned to her hut, and Mother Granchelli returned to the farm where she began preparing dinner for Papa. She would not talk about what she had seen, what she had heard, or what she had done. That was something private meant to be kept between the two strong women—the traveler and the settler.

Larry checked his phone for the umpteenth time to see the progress of the hurricane. It was stationary directly over Raleigh. The National Weather Service couldn't yet determine how long it would remain in its current position or which direction it would take once it started to move again.

The last message he received from Carolina was that everyone was going to a safe area in the basement of the dormitory to wait out the storm. That was good.

The other message he had received from her was something about Lyuba warning her about a key and a seraphim. That was not good. He could understand if Lyuba was warning her about the storm. But warning her about a key and a seraphim didn't make sense; he didn't know what it meant, and that worried him.

As the son of the gypsy king, he had grown up in the gypsy traditions. He had learned much and still respected if not held on to many of the travelers' beliefs. But he didn't understand what Lyuba meant by a key or a seraphim. If the *choovihni* was warning Carolina, it had to be serious. He tried calling Carolina, but couldn't get through.

He checked his watch; he was already late for his next class.

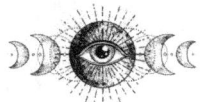

Milosh was hot and sweaty. The place where he was digging, removed from everyone else and in front of the cave's entrance, was directly in the sun; plus he could feel the sand in his clothing irritating his skin. The others were probably laughing at him for picking that spot to dig. If he moved, though, it would show that he was weak. He wouldn't do that, no matter how hot it was or how itchy his skin got.

The more uncomfortable he felt, the angrier he became, and all of his anger was directed toward Lyuba. He knew she was vulnerable when it came to her daughter, Carolina, and those brash three young women. All of them settlers. They didn't know the ways of the gypsies, and they didn't show respect. At least not to him when they came barging into the *Kaulo Camio* camp looking for the *choovihni*.

His curse had almost worked before, but he had only

been a boy then. Now he was a man. He would make it stronger the next time. He still had the jar that held poisonous herbs he had stolen from Lyuba's shelf, and the strands of baby hair he had found in the framed picture she had on a table in her hut. He also had the old book of curses that belonged to the Bandoleer. He had been studying the book; he had learned a lot. The next time he wouldn't fail. Wiping the sweat from his face, he grabbed his small trowel and angrily stabbed at the earth.

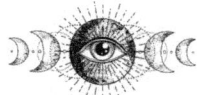

Dara, being the tallest of the F.I.G.s and the most aggressive, spoke first. "O.K., let's think about what Lyuba said—exactly."

Carolina repeated the message just as Mrs. Ball and Miss Alcott had relayed it: *They must seek safe shelter. When the leaves twist on their stems away from the heavens to face the earth, they must hide. You must hide. Everyone is in danger.*

*When the seraphim sings, a key will be given to her; she needs to listen for the seraphim's song. She needs to watch for the key and protect it from evil. She must return it to where it belongs.*

"The storm must be the danger," said Jennifer, "but what key?"

"I have a key to my bungalow and my car key," said Carolina. "I don't think that is what Lyuba means though."

"A seraphim is an angel referenced in the book of the Prophet Isaiah in the bible," offered Mackenzie, picking up on the words *seraphim's song*. "It is the angel that allows people on earth and the gods in the heavens to communicate, and it is a copper color."

"In Hebrew the word *seraphim* means *burning* or *fiery*," added Dara.

"That must refer to its color," said Jennifer.

"How can I protect it and return it to where it belongs if I don't even know what it is?" Carolina was still thinking about a key.

"And what does Milosh have to do with it?" Dara looked at the others. They had no answers, only questions.

Outside the storm continued to rage. Wind battered the three-storied stone building; beyond the stone walls, trees toppled and structures collapsed; and streets flooded from the relentless down-pouring of rain. But Carolina and the females of intellectual genius, deep in thought, no longer noticed.

Suddenly Jennifer jumped up and grabbed the canvas board she had been drawing on with her charcoals. The last image that had come to her was an object of some sort, cylinder in shape, and an unusual shade of yellow. She showed it to the others. "This is what I am working on now. These are the images I have been seeing." She pointed to the dark swirls and the yellow cylinder. "What if it isn't a regular key as we think of it—like a door key—but something else, like a metaphor?"

Dara immediately began thinking of phrases where

the word "key" could be used. "Like *keyed up, minor and major key, key out, key to happiness, key to success…*"

"Or, *key to information,*" said Jennifer looking at her charcoal images. "What if it is some sort of object like an ancient artifact that deciphers information?" She cocked her head, listening. "And I keep hearing the key of B flat minor. At least that is what I think it is because it is slightly off tune."

"Yeah," said Mackenzie. "Maybe it is something that connects language, math, and music," which might explain why her thoughts lately had focused on the relationship between musical scales and mathematical equations. "The ancient Chinese, Indians, Egyptians and even Mesopotamians were known to have studied the mathematical principles of sound, and the Pythagoreans of ancient Greece were the first researchers known to have investigated the expression of musical scales in terms of numerical ratios. They believed that all nature consists of harmony arising out of numbers."

"Lyuba said I must watch for the key, so that means I must not have it yet." Carolina looked at Jennifer. "I have been hearing that musical note as well. It is the same sound as 'aum' that is used in meditation and religious practices all over the world. Maybe that is the seraphim's song."

"And the vibrations… Have any of you been feeling the vibrations?" asked Dara.

Carolina, Mackenzie, and Jennifer all nodded.

Dara reached into her backpack and pulled out a

notebook and several loose papers. "This is what I have been working on," she said, showing them the sheets of paper where she had written down symbols and other strange markings. "It isn't any language known to man as far as I can tell. I am convinced it is something that was used before any known civilization existed—here on earth."

"What are you saying, Dara? 'Here on earth.'" Mackenzie moved a little closer to Jennifer.

"I think it might be a language from another world, another planet or galaxy, or maybe even the gods themselves."

Anyone listening to their conversation, anyone other than the F.I.G.s, would have laughed at the ridiculousness of it all. But these young women were Carolina and the three females of intellectual genius. They didn't laugh because there was nothing ridiculous about it. They believed in one another and, therefore, they believed what each one was saying. It didn't matter if it sounded ridiculous or not.

Just then there was a loud thump. Carolina looked around and saw the headmaster getting up off the floor and putting his cot upright the way it should be. He had apparently been dozing and then fallen off his cot. He wasn't hurt, but the frame of the cot was slightly bent which made the thing wobbly when he sat on it. "Nothing broken," he said grinning and totally embarrassed when he saw them looking his way. Miss Alcott and Mrs. Ball glanced at each other and giggled.

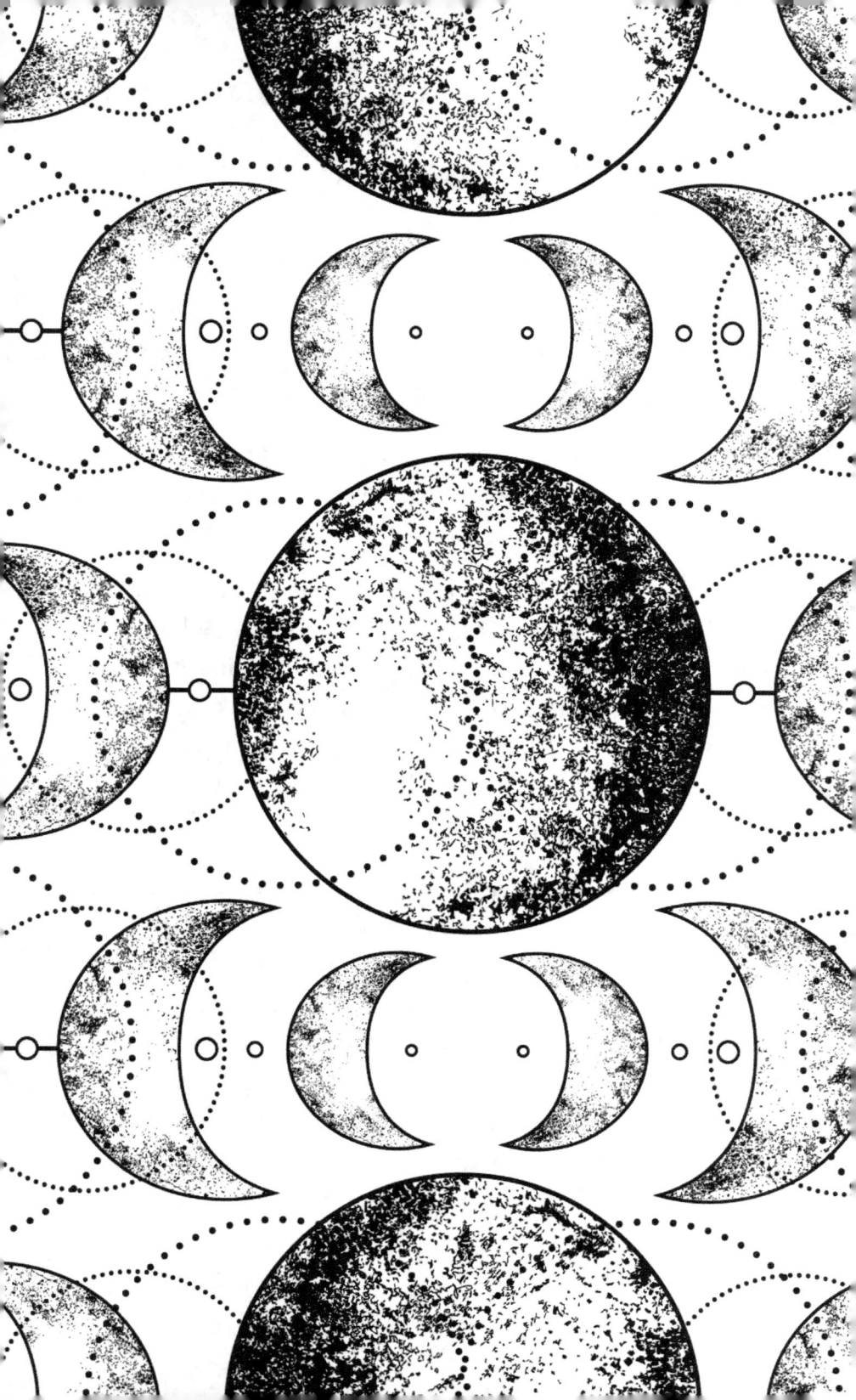

# CHAPTER 11

Dr. Stanwick squatted in front of the mouth of the cave staring into its vast empty darkness, his shock of white hair shone like a beacon of light in the bright fullness of the moon. Always the last to leave at the end of the day, this was the quiet time he set aside to review in his mind what had been accomplished during the day, what new discoveries had been made, and make plans for what needed to be done the following day.

Never married, his work was what he loved, and he had dedicated his entire life to it. Even as a child he had been interested in archaeology, visiting museums, reading thick texts of the world's greatest discoveries. The oldest known human footprints found in North America that were twenty-nine track marks believed to be over 13,000 years old; the world's largest Buddhist temple in Borobudur, India, built in the ninth century; the lost Trojan city of Tenea; Knossos, believed to have been settled in the Neolithic period and Europe's oldest city—the young Richard Stanwick had read about all of them. When he began his studies at the University of York and then later at the University of Oxford, England, he narrowed his passion to the study of archaeology in China and that is where it remained.

Known as a plodder, throughout his career he had rejected the lure of the splashy, news-worthy digs, those well-known excavations that would draw major funding and universal recognition such as the terracotta soldiers found in the Shaanxi province which dated to the first dynasty. He preferred to follow his passion to the unknown or lesser-known sites in China, and restoring to life and memory that which had become insignificant and long-ago forgotten. It was through this work that he received the most joy and personal fulfillment. Accolades could go to others as far as he was concerned. His mission was to save what remained from the past for the future.

He would soon turn 69 years old. This dig would be his last before being forced into retirement. The wear and tear on his body through the years of difficult travel to undiscovered parts of the world, the physical demands of digging impossible sites in all kinds of inclement weather, sleeping in tents or simply on the ground out in the open, and eating whatever was easy and available at the time or place had taken its toll.

Through it all, he had held close the stories from his childhood about a key that could open a portal between heaven and earth in a mysterious land where the early gypsies had first settled—not in Europe as everyone believed, but in China.

Others dismissed the stories as myth and fantasy, but it was his belief that most myths were based on truths. There was an increasing amount of evidence to support that belief. The city of Troy as described in Homer's *Iliad* and believed to be fictitious had been discovered in Hisarlik, Turkey. The *Mahabharata*, one of two Sanskrit epochs, describes Dvaraka in India, what was once believed to be a mythical historic city with over 900,000 palaces. However, in 2001, archaeological evidence from onshore and offshore excavations confirmed that Dvaraka really existed.

Even in the Christian bible, the story of God commanding Joshua to destroy Jericho was once believed to be myth. However, archaeologists had discovered a city on the west bank of Palestine fitting its description. Most recently, there was even evidence that the lost continent of Atlantis had been located near New Zealand.

More often than not, archaeologists were discovering that ancient writings of places and things weren't myth or fantasy at all, but real and based on fact. It was the reason he had decided to become an archaeologist. Dr. Len Wu, an old friend and colleague, agreed with him. He would be bringing a brilliant young woman named Dara Roux to visit the site in a few weeks. It would be interesting to see their reaction to what he had discovered so far.

If he could prove that the gypsies had originally settled in the area of the Luoli Project site, and the reason was because that is where a key making possible the communication between man and the gods was found, it would be the biggest discovery since Howard Carter's excavation in Egypt at the Valley of the Kings in 1922 resulting in locating Tutankhamun's tomb, or Hiram Bingham's 1911 finding the Machu Picchu in Peru. It would be the perfect culmination of his interesting but somewhat lackluster and not particularly memorable career.

When he was first given financing for the Luoli Project, even though slight, it was a dream come true. After that, it had taken eighteen months to secure the necessary permissions from the Chinese government to excavate; then another two months to find qualified people to work the site. And there were restrictions. They had been given only eight months to complete their work. Then he would have to go through the process again. He wasn't sure he had the strength or stamina. His body was telling him that he didn't.

Early indications showing this area near the Yellow Sea being settled by gypsies were promising. There had been interesting finds of pottery, tools, and other things that were definitely not of Chinese origin. Each of these artifacts he had carefully cleaned, examined, and catalogued for further evaluation.

As interesting as these discoveries were, however, his instincts were telling him there was a great deal more still to be found, things of great importance, maybe even the key from the stories he remembered as a young boy. But it meant exploring the cave that the locals called *jinzhi de*, or forbidden. It was the cave of the pig dragon, according to Chinese legend, and the Chinese people refused to enter it.

Early the next morning he was planning to go into the city of Puli and meet with officials in charge of the Department of Regional Antiquities and Archaeological Studies. He hoped to be able to convince them to provide more funding that would pay for the additional equipment he would need to go into the cave, as well as more workers who didn't believe in the pig dragon. Without it, he feared the Luoli Project would fail.

"What secrets do you guard?" he whispered into the

night. His body stiff and aching, he stood with difficulty and approached the mouth of the cave. Why did the gypsies choose this of all places those many centuries ago? The dust devils alone made living conditions almost inhabitable, and the yellow clay soil starved of nutrients was not conducive for growing crops. There were so many other areas that would have been better suited. Yet he was convinced they had made this area their home, and it had something to do with the mysterious cave. More than ever, he was determined to discover what it was.

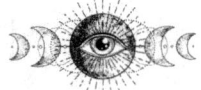

All through the night and into the next day Lyuba studied the Tarot. As the darkness turned to light and night into day, the cards slowly revealed themselves. The card showing strength, the Lion; the Wheel of Fortune, indicating change; and then the card of Death, only in this case indicating the end of something in this life in order to make room for something new. She revealed the next two cards: the Tower meaning an unexpected blow; the Star of Luck and hope for future happiness. And then, the last card, Temperance. Her daughter would need to be watchful and take special care.

Relying on her instinctive psychic powers, she selected two cards from those which had not yet been chosen. The first was the Seven of Wands. There were difficulties ahead requiring all of her daughter's endurance and strength to overcome. The other was the World card. Lyuba smiled. Carolina would face a difficult challenge, but in the end, she would prevail.

She turned to the crystal. Her thoughts were of her daughter, Carolina, and the three young women. As she searched the crystal, the answers she received only took her so far into the future and then went dark.

She knew the danger of the storm would pass; and Carolina would receive the key. But there was more which remained hidden. It was the terrible evil festering within Milosh that most frightened her. She would not rest until she knew what form that evil would take and what path. She had to understand how it would materialize and how it would manifest. Only then would she know how she could fight it.

As the sun rose higher in the sky, there was much activity around the camp. The crows gave warning first, then the starlings. The dogs were the last to give notice to the travelers that someone was approaching. It was the excited notice of recognition; it was someone with a familiar scent—someone who belonged.

The Bandoleer had been gone for several days and was now returning. After resting, he would have much to tell the gypsies of his tribe about the different places he had visited and potential new markets where they could sell their wares. Rather than go to his hut, however, he went to the hut belonging to the *choovihni*. There he stood outside, quietly and respectfully, waiting to be invited in.

Lyuba sensed the Bandoleer's presence and opened her door to him. Once inside they sat at the table where only moments earlier she had been reading the Tarot and what she called scrying into the crystal ball.

"I have unfortunate news," the Bandoleer said. "While traveling, I visited many other camps and other tribes. I was told that Milosh visited the same camps—the same tribes—asking to stay. He was turned away. He has a book—a book of curses—my book that was passed down to me."

Lyuba understood the meaning behind the Bandoleer's words. Milosh would use the curse again to seek revenge against her. He would try to harm Carolina. His *chakra* was still brown. It always would be.

"I learned that he has gone to where it all began for our people. The *Zep Tepi*—the first time," he said, referring to the ancient Egyptian creation myth.

"The *jinzhi de* cave," said Lyuba.

The Bandoleer nodded.

Lyuba reached out and touched the hand of this strong man who was the leader of the *Kaulo Camio* tribe, knowing his heart was aching, knowing the pain and grief he was experiencing to tell her the things he did. He of all people knew what it meant. Yet the outcome was already fixed. It had been predetermined when Milosh was born. It was both his destiny and his demise.

The Bandoleer would be able to survive losing his only child—a son. In his mind, he had already lost him when Milosh was banned from the tribe. The Bandoleer's wife, Djidjo, would not. Through the years she had turned away from the truth about her son, and in many ways enabled the wickedness that festered within him. The price she would pay would be heavy.

After he left, Lyuba returned to the cemetery located next to the creek. She needed some of the flowers and herbs she respected but normally left alone and undisturbed. Delphinium, bloodroot, oleander, and the bishop's weed. She needed to use all of her power and wisdom if she was to save Carolina.

She understood now what the Tarot and crystal had been telling her. Milosh had found the key and done something to it causing everything past, present, and future to become unbalanced. And he intended to destroy her by taking away Carolina. Once again, he would place a curse of death on her daughter.

The category 5 hurricane named Luoli raged through the night and by morning there was still no indication of it letting up. Wind speeds were being recorded above 157 miles per hour, the highest strength indicated on the Saffir-Simpson Hurricane Wind Scale. No one slept in the safe area of the dormitory basement and tempers were starting to show in small ways.

Dr. Connoly, professor of physics and chemistry, got into a rather loud verbal exchange with the two new professors over the last package of peanut butter crackers that was left on the food and drink table. Clyde Benson, weary of Dr. Sullivan's mindless ramblings of aliens, hurt her feelings when he crossly told her it was all a bunch of claptrap and to just shut up. Others simply withdrew, as though into a shell, wishing they were invisible, preferring to just be left alone.

Then, as quickly as it had appeared, it disappeared. All inside the safe room and outside became quiet and still. The wind stopped wailing, the rain stopped falling, thick clouds thinned and darkened skies cleared, and the leaves on the trees once again turned upward toward the heavens and the sun shining brightly in the sky. The fearful noise of the howling destructive winds and unrelenting downpour of rain was suddenly replaced by an eerie unbroken silence. Then, within moments, the silence was also replaced, and the happy sound of singing birds could be heard.

Everyone in the basement was eager to leave the safe area and see what damage had been left by the storm. And they wanted to return to what had been normal in their lives as quickly as possible—before Luoli.

Outside, they were amazed to find only some broken limbs scattered haphazardly around the wide grassy area of lawn. Other than that, there appeared to be no damage to any of the buildings or even the vehicles owned by the faculty and staff that had been parked by each of the bungalows.

First and foremost in Carolina's mind was to help Jimmy Bob look for Tick. "The girls and I will drive around the area to see if we can find him," she told Jimmy Bob. "You might want to take a good look around your family home. He might have gone there since it is a place he knows." Before she and the F.I.G.s could get into her car, however, they were surprised to see a police patrol car slowly approaching with blue lights flashing.

The patrolman was Hank Pollock, a long-time friend of Jimmy Bob's who occasionally visited Wood Rose and had helped out at various fund-raising events for the orphanage throughout the years. Walking in front of the patrol car carrying in his mouth what appeared to be a very large muddy bone was Tick. Slowly and deliberately, unscathed and completely ignoring the vehicle with its flashing blue lights behind him, Wood Rose's guard dog didn't stop until he got to Carolina. Then, somewhat ceremoniously, he dropped the dirt-covered object at her feet.

Jimmy Bob was beside himself with joy as he tearfully knelt down hugging his much-loved canine who had somehow managed to survive the strongest, most terrifying hurricane in recorded history.

"I saw him up on the road headed this way and tried to get him in the vehicle, but he didn't want to ride I guess," Hank said. "I think he was afraid I was going to try to take that bone he had in his mouth away from him." He watched the dog for a moment. "Looks like he wants you to have it," he said glancing at Carolina.

Jennifer gasped as the pain in her chest returned. Then the musical notes of a tone poem that only she could hear rapidly filled the blank measures, treble and bass clef she saw in her mind. Just beneath the musical notes, loud and insistent, refusing to be ignored, was the relentless, continuous undertone of the key B flat minor. The "aum."

Dara looked up into the sky and envisioned words, symbols, and pictures of unknown origin, from another universe—another galaxy, yet she felt she knew their meaning. She understood.

And flashes of mathematical formula involving units, intervals, and spacing of the solar system penetrated Mackenzie's mind as she removed her calculator from her belt and began entering mathematical equations representing what she saw.

Carolina squeezed her eyes shut; the tone of B flat minor was almost deafening. Then, because the vibration of the earth was so strong, the four young women knelt to the ground holding each other to keep from falling.

Jimmy Bob and Hank steadied themselves. "Must be having an earthquake," Hank said looking around. No sooner than he said the words, it then stopped.

As Tick continued to watch Carolina, she suddenly heard her mother's voice—soft, but clear and urgent. *It is the key, daughter. You must protect it and return it to the cave.*

The F.I.G.s couldn't hear Lyuba—only Carolina could hear her—but they knew. Carolina had been given the key, she must keep it safe, and she must return it to where it belonged.

They also knew, because they were females of intellectual genius, that Carolina was in danger, and they didn't know what to do to stop it. They didn't know how to help her. And this more than anything terrified them.

Carolina reached down and patted Tick on his head. "Did you bring this to me, Tick?" Her thoughts turned to the strange pattern of cots, chairs, tables, and people she had noticed earlier from the stairs leading down into the safe room—the Canis Major constellation. "You are the Dog Star, Tick, the brightest star in the night sky heavens." She cradled his face in her hands and stroked his long silky ears. "Good boy. Such a good boy." Only when she picked the object up did he acknowledge Jimmy Bob with big, wet slurpy kisses and soft grunts that sounded more like a pig than Wood Rose's brave guard dog.

The storm had knocked some trees down on White Oak Road near the Five Points area, according to Hank, and there were some downed power lines near the Capitol building leaving some without electricity. But overall, they had been fortunate not to have suffered any more damage than they did. As far as he knew, there had been no injuries reported.

A grounds crew came later that afternoon and under Jimmy Bob's direction cleaned up the campus from what mess and debris had been left by the storm. Before leaving, they also helped Ms. Larkins put all of the cots, tables, and chairs back into storage. With no other storm issues to deal with, by nightfall everything looked and felt normal; everyone returned to what they had been doing before Lu-oli came.

It seemed as though there hadn't even been a storm, or at the most it had simply been a bad dream. Normal activities resumed, and all was as it should be at Wood Rose Orphanage and Academy for Young Women.

Almost.

Dara, Mackenzie, and Jennifer were exhausted and they were scared. Something dangerous and urgent was taking place. The storm was only a part of it. It involved Carolina, but they didn't know what, other than Milosh was somehow also a part of it.

They remembered how Carolina had almost died before from his curse when they were staying at the Granchelli farm in Frascati, Italy, how she couldn't wake up from the fever, and the only one who could save her was Lyuba because she was a *choovihni*.

They remembered the dried herbs mixed with oils, the tea extracts made from asparagus and olive leaves, and the handkerchief soaked in a bowl of egg whites then wrapped around Carolina's feet, but even with all of this, Carolina's fever didn't break. It was only after Lyuba performed a ritual that only she would know—because she was a *choovihni*—that Carolina was saved.

But this time they weren't in Frascati, Italy, and Lyuba and her *Kaulo Camio* tribe weren't camped nearby. The F.I.G.s went to their bungalow—their forever home. They would start fresh early the next morning after they had a chance to rest. There had to be some way to figure it all out.

# CHAPTER 12

Carolina carried Tick's bone to her bungalow and left it next to the kitchen sink, too tired at that moment to do anything else with it. She and her girls would study it more closely the next day after they had gotten some sleep.

Carolina tried to call Larry. When he didn't answer, she left a message letting him know they were all right. The storm had passed. There had been some trees and electrical lines downed and some flooding around the city, but Wood Rose had been left relatively untouched.

She didn't mention the object Tick had brought to her or the new warnings she had been getting from Lyuba. She would tell him when he called later that evening when they could talk in person. Besides, she was frightened and she didn't want him to know just how much. He would only worry. Maybe by waiting to talk to him, she would know more about what was going on. Maybe by then she would have learned more from Lyuba and she wouldn't be so scared.

She unloaded the groceries she had bought earlier before the storm from her car. As she was putting everything away, Miss Alcott and Mrs. Ball stopped in so Miss Alcott could give her the things she had in the trunk of Mrs. Ball's car that included several sealed boxes with the word

*PRECIOUS* written on them in purple ink. Carolina was speechless. "How can I ever thank you, Miss Alcott."

Most of the things Carolina decorated her bungalow with had come from thrift stores and antique shops. The things Miss Alcott had given her were so much nicer than anything she had. She would never have been able to afford them.

Miss Alcott told her about each thing, giving her a little history of what it was, where it had come from, and how she had gotten it: a floor vase with a painted pastoral scene that had come from Vienna—a trip she had made with a friend; a chocolate pot with hand painted pink and yellow roses and eight matching cups from England—another trip with the same friend; an abstract painting of brightly colored animals by the famous German artist Franz Marc—given to her by her father; jewelry that had been passed down to her from her mother and grandmother; leather-bound books—first editions that had been her uncle's; a set of china that served twelve that had belonged to a favorite aunt; crystal glasses; sets of sterling silverware; and so much more.

"You and the F.I.G.s are my family now, so I want you to have the photographs," she said, giving her the box that held several photograph albums. "I know you won't know most of the people, but I still want you to have them." Hesitating, she gently brushed her hand over one of the albums, almost caressing it, like a loving gesture of saying goodbye. "One day they might mean something to you." Then pointing to the sealed boxes, she only said, "You can open those at another time."

When the ladies left, Carolina stacked the sealed boxes along with the photograph albums in a closet. The boxes and albums carried the scent of roses, lavender, and honeysuckle, probably from sachets. She would look through them later.

Not ready to settle down, too tired to sleep, she started placing the other things throughout the rooms of her three-bedroom home, loving each priceless object Miss Alcott had given her. She found a perfect place for everything, and everything looked as though it had always belonged.

The beautiful jewelry she kept in their velvet cases and put them in a dresser drawer. She would wear different pieces whenever she and Larry had something special to celebrate or somewhere special to go. And when Larry got back from Buenos Aires, they must invite Miss Alcott and Mrs. Ball over for a nice dinner one evening. She would use some of the beautiful fine china Miss Alcott had given to her and pick out something from the velvet jewelry cases to wear. The F.I.G.s, of course, would be invited too.

Before showering and going to bed, Carolina looked once more at the object Tick had given to her. She didn't want to disturb too much of the caked yellow soil on it until the F.I.G.s were there with her, but she did notice a place where the dirt, or what looked like clay, had fallen off or maybe it had been scraped off. From what she could see, it didn't look like a bone.

She got a clean kitchen towel from the drawer and carefully wrapped the object in it. Then she put it on her small table next to her bed. She couldn't stop thinking about Tick and what he had done. What he must have gone through. She knew that what had happened—the storm, Tick getting lost and then bringing her this object—was almost other worldly. The object or "key"—whatever it was—had to be important. It was the reason everything seemed out of balance.

Her mother had told her to protect it from evil and return it to where it belonged—wherever that was. Worried that something might happen to it, she took it off her bedside table and put it under her pillow where it would be close to her as she slept. She felt frustrated because she and the F.I.G.s hadn't been able to come up with a plan. They just didn't know enough yet. And she was frightened, and she didn't even know why other than Lyuba had said the name of Milosh.

Carolina hadn't been able to see the danger before when Milosh put a curse on her. She hadn't known how to protect herself. Now, she still didn't know. Hopefully, with the storm moving back out to sea, Lyuba would be able to send her more information.

Just before Larry called, she heard her mother say the word *jinzhi de.*

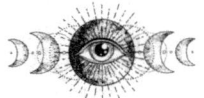

Lying in the middle of her bed, the covers neatly folded back, Dara started remembering. Things that she thought she had hidden away in the darkest corners of her mind now surfaced making it impossible for her to sleep.

Memories of always feeling hungry and the pungent odor of swamp mud. Her mama wearing bright red lipstick. There was only her and her mama, and she learned at a young age what she needed to do to survive. For her, survival had come by way of foreign, obscure, and obsolete languages picked up from all of the men wearing white military uniforms who had visited her mama. Learning them, understanding them, making them her constant companions. There was nothing she couldn't interpret, decipher or translate.

They had a small garden, she remembered, but nothing much ever came of it, and there was an old, smoke-blackened pot sitting out front in the yard that her mama burned kerosene in to keep the snakes away. Home was a rusted-out trailer set back in a thicket near a ditch bank that usually flooded whenever it rained.

Thinking back on it now in the darkness of her room, Dara no longer remembered what the inside of the trailer looked like—they couldn't have had much. She only remembered her and her mama sitting on the outside stoop listening to tree frogs and cicadas while muddy flood waters lapped at their bare feet.

Dara hadn't known fear then as a young child. Even when her mother left her in the store and never came back for her she wasn't afraid. And later, living at Wood Rose, nothing intimidated her. She could stand up for herself with the best of them, including Thurgood, the headmaster. But now, sensing that something was again threatening Carolina, she didn't know what to do about it. She didn't know how to stand up against it, and she was terrified. She didn't know what to do about that either. *"Shekoo, baboo!"* she said out loud into the darkness, words of profanity from an ancient dialect.

Mackenzie sat up in her bed working with her calculator with her foot sticking out from the covers like a barometer. When Carolina came to Wood Rose, for the first time in her life Mackenzie actually knew what happiness felt like. She felt like she as a person mattered, and the things she said, even if sometimes they weren't said well, were important. All of her unspoken dreams suddenly became a reality under Carolina's tutelage.

Then, finding her mother and working in a field of research where she could use numbers was more wonderful than she ever could have imagined. It gave her a sense of accomplishment and success. And it was all because of Carolina. But something terrible was about to happen, and it involved Carolina. She just didn't know what it was, and the fear she had always felt when growing up had come back. Only this time it was much worse.

Tears spilled from her eyes as she brushed her fingers through her short brown hair in frustration. All of her life Mackenzie had been afraid—afraid of not living up to what was expected of her, afraid of leaving behind something or someone—or being left. So she focused on those things she enjoyed the most and caused the least amount of criticism. Even at a very young age, that focus was on numbers. They were her friends. She loved them—playing with them, seeing how many ways she could make them relate to each other in unusual ways and relate to her. And like friends, at night when it was time to put them away, she would say good-bye before she went to sleep. *Good-bye, cofactor matrix. Good-bye, antipodal points. Good-bye, 3.*

The simple, natural number 3 was her favorite for some unknown reason. She agreed with the Greek mathematician Pythagoras that it was the noblest of all numbers. She liked its simplicity and the fact that it was the only number written as three lines in Roman and Chinese numerals, as well as the Brahmin Indian and the Gupta, although the Gupta made their lines more curved.

Perhaps it was her favorite, however, because it made her think of a father, mother, and child. It was the trinity, the troika. It was the family she had never known until Carolina, Dara, and Jennifer helped her find out who her father and mother were. It was the three females of intellectual genius—and Carolina.

She punched more numbers into the calculator. There was a connection between music, language, and the mathematical formula she created involving units, intervals, and spacing of the solar system. That was why Jennifer was hearing the note of B flat minor and why Dara was seeing words and symbols and pictures that seemed to be from another universe. As unrelated and disconnected as they were, there was a certain mathematical logic to it. For some reason, though, she just couldn't find it. She couldn't see the numerical pattern.

Numbers had never failed her; they had been her friends from the time she could hold a pencil. The idea that they couldn't help her now when Carolina's life might depend on it was more than her fragile emotions could comprehend.

When her tears turned to sobs, she turned off her calculator and tiptoed into Dara's room. "Come on, get in," said Dara, as though she had expected her.

Carefully, trying not to wrinkle the covers that had been neatly folded back, Mackenzie climbed into bed with another female of intellectual genius, poking her foot out from the covers like a barometer.

Believing that her parents had been tragically killed in an automobile accident, and with a little over a year to go before she could be considered an adult and live on her own, Jennifer had been placed at the Wood Rose Orphanage and Academy for Young Women. There were no other family members, at least none who would take in the brilliant but explosively unpredictable young teenager.

Wood Rose supposedly had an excellent music department and art department, both nationally recognized, she was assured, where she could continue her studies. The "excellent" music and art departments, however, weren't prepared for the young genius. Moody and prone to emotional outbursts, at 16 years of age Jennifer possessed more talent than the six faculty members making up the two departments put together.

It would have been a disaster if it hadn't been for Dara and Mackenzie. Like Jennifer, they also were considered different—because they were. They understood what it was like to try to communicate on a level where others would understand, but not succeed. To want to be included, but feeling resentful because they never were and, after all, what difference did it make? To want desperately to be like everyone else, but knowing that was impossible—because they weren't.

Jennifer immediately fit in as a FIG. When her temper got out of control, it was Dara who could calm her. When she needed space and solitude because the pictures filling her head had changed into so many musical notes that she couldn't write them down fast enough, Mackenzie understood and protected her. For a while, they just had each other—the three of them—females of intellectual genius. F.I.G.s. Then Carolina came. Instinctively they knew Carolina was one of them, and they loved her for it.

Now, in the quiet of her room, Jennifer concentrated on the dark images she had drawn on her canvas board and the musical notes and harmonics that were written on the pages of eight-stave paper strewn all over her bed. A tone poem. It was a symphonic poem written as a single-movement orchestral piece, and it was telling a story of something hidden, yet revealing—an ancient artifact that held the answers to all that was, is, and will be.

Still she didn't understand. What was it saying? What was its meaning? As she heard the dissonant musical notes, she rapidly wrote them down, measure after measure, switching from *accarezzevole*—caressing and expressive—to *agitato*—agitated. When more images filled her mind, she drew on her canvas board, adding more yellow and purple, more definition and illumination.

And when there were no longer notes to hear or images to see, she became panicked. She still hadn't found any answers to help Carolina. Not knowing what else to do, she stomped into Dara's room and stood at the foot of the bed. "Get in," said Dara.

Jennifer flipped her long blond ponytail and climbed into Dara's bed, pushing Mackenzie over and not bothering with straightening the covers. There in the darkness, with so many unanswered questions and "what ifs," their concern for Carolina almost unbearable, their minds finally quieted and three females of intellectual genius slept at last.

# CHAPTER 13

Milosh got to the camp just before daylight. Dr. Stanwick had said he would be gone all day; therefore, the workers were on their own. By getting there early, Milosh could go into the cave before the others arrived. That way no one would know he was even there, and he would be able to spend all day exploring in the cave. Later, he would go to the apothecary shop in Puli to get the herbs he needed: snakeroot, areca nut, bitter orange, dyer's whin—he had studied all of them, and he knew which ones were the most potent and had the most devastating effect. This time he would not fail.

With his digging tools and a flashlight, he first checked the area where he had found the large artifact that had the engraved symbols and writing. He hoped to find another one, or at least other things that were similar. The bigger, the better. It was the large ones that commanded the most money.

There were piles of rocks on the ground near a large fissure in the wall of the cave where he had first found the cylinder deeply wedged. The jagged opening which had exposed the cylinder had probably been caused by an earthquake, and he had made the opening larger when he pried the object from its hiding place. He didn't see anything else of interest, so he made his way deeper into the cave where he hadn't explored before.

What sounded like wind surprised him, at first hardly noticeable, then louder the deeper he went. He wondered if there might be another opening into the cave somewhere. He would look for that another time. Right now he just wanted to find as many artifacts as he could so he could sell them.

At the end of the day as it was almost dark, Milosh returned to the cave's entrance dragging his bag of newly-found artifacts. The effort had been worth it. There was evidence that people had actually lived in the cave and not just nearby close to the shoreline of the Yellow Sea. Gypsies. In addition to smaller broken clay fragments and pieces of metal implements or tools, he had found several small bowls in perfect condition, and large drinking or maybe storage vessels. They might even be ceremonial vessels similar to those used in state rituals. Some of them had cracks, but they would still fetch a high price.

He hoisted the heavy bag over his shoulder. Knowing everyone would already be gone at the camp, he walked out of the cave and directly into a startled Dr. Richard Stanwick.

"Milosh!" Dr. Stanwick looked at the bag, the tools and flashlight he was carrying, and knew instantly what Milosh had done.

Knowing it was obvious to Dr. Stanwick why he was exiting the cave with a heavy bag, Milosh got defensive and tried to lie his way out of it. "I knew no one else would go into the cave, so I thought I would check it out."

It was a lame excuse and he knew it, but he couldn't come up with anything else. One of the first rules Dr. Stanwick had instructed him on when searching for artifacts was to document where the artifact had been found, make a drawing of the area, and make notes of everything about it. He had done none of that; therefore, he had contaminated the findings and most likely the cave.

Dr. Stanwick was furious. He snatched the bag off Milosh's shoulder and opened it. When he saw what was inside, he felt sick. The finds could have been enough to convince the officials in charge of Regional Antiquities and Archaeological Studies to give him the funding he so desperately needed. "I want you off this site now, and don't come back." He grabbed the tools and flashlight he had given Milosh to use when he first hired him. "And I want you out of that trailer by sunrise tomorrow."

Milosh glared at Dr. Stanwick. "If I were you, I'd be careful, old man, or you might find yourself in a place where you don't want to be." Threatening, fists clenched in anger, Milosh turned away cocky and full of himself. He could do anything he wanted because he had the Bandoleer's book of curses.

Dr. Stanwick had suspected that Milosh might be stealing artifacts to sell on the black market, but he didn't have any evidence to prove that was the reason Milosh had asked for a job other than his obvious lack of experience. Unfortunately, it was a common problem in archaeology. Now, this.

Shaking his head, he carefully carried the bag of artifacts to his truck. He would take them with him for safe-keeping in case Milosh decided to come back, then bring them to the site the next morning and try to sort through them. If nothing else, he could truthfully claim that they had been found in the *jinzhi de* cave.

The meeting earlier in the day with officials in charge of Regional Antiquities and Archaeological Studies hadn't gone that well. They were courteous and attentive to his proposal and request for more funding, but he didn't sense there was any enthusiasm for the Luoli Project. They said they would give him their decision in about a week. Until then, he would just have to keep positive thoughts.

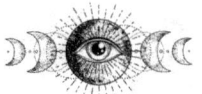

When Dara, Mackenzie, and Jennifer arrived at Carolina's early the next morning, she served them from the beautiful chocolate pot decorated with pink and yellow roses and matching cups that Miss Alcott had given to her. "She got them in England when she went there with a friend," Carolina told them. Feeling more rested than they had the day before, they drank the hot chocolate and then turned their attention to "Tick's bone," as she and her girls decided to call it.

When she told Larry about what had happened before going to bed the night before, he advised her to not try to clean it with anything more than water and a soft brush. Not knowing what it was made of, it was better to err on the side of caution.

Carolina carefully unwrapped the bone and carried it to the kitchen sink. Dara looked closely at the yellow dirt. "You know what this looks like? It reminds me of that place where Mackenzie's mother—Ling—took us. The place where they think gypsies might have settled. Remember? I noticed then how yellow the soil was—clay actually."

"That's right," said Mackenzie.

"I got it all over my shoes," said Jennifer, "and it was really hard to get off."

Dara continued to study the bone. "There is a new archaeological site nearby called the Luoli Project, and that is where Dr. Wu plans to take me to visit when I go back to China."

"Luoli? That is the same name as the hurricane," said Carolina.

"The name that means *gypsy*," said Dara.

Carolina gently started brushing the dirt, getting some of the larger chunks off. When the brush no longer did any good, she dampened some paper towels and carefully wiped it. "Well, it definitely isn't bone," she said after a while. She held it up to the light. "I think it is crystal."

"Crystals have their own unique vibration," said Dara, "and it is constant—like a constant frequency. So that means crystals can realign and re-calibrate your energy with theirs, helping you to raise your vibration and reach a higher state of being.

"Einstein and other scientists believed that crystals

can store energy as well as information." She paused, thinking, "They also believed that crystals know intentions and it is possible for crystals to react to intentions."

"My gosh." Jennifer leaned forward to get a better look at the object. "That must mean that if someone tried to do damage to it, it might react somehow in a negative way."

"Milosh," whispered Mackenzie.

Carolina kept rubbing, and more details began to emerge. The most obvious were the lines of etched symbols, symbols similar to what Dara had been seeing. She carried it wrapped in the towel into the living room and put it on the table in front of the sofa where they could examine it more closely.

"*Shekoo, baboo!*" said Dara.

"What is it, Dara?" Carolina handed Tick's bone to her. "Can you read it?"

"Some of it." She turned it so she could see all of the sides and angles. "It is similar to the ancient languages of Sanskrit and that of the Persians, but yet it is different. I think it is earlier—a lot earlier. Maybe even prehistory." After studying it a while she placed it back on the towel. "It seems to be some sort of device that translates musical vibrations mathematically into a language. A written and spoken language."

"Like the pitches of notes and the tempo of pulse as it relates to the measurement of mathematical time and frequency," said Mackenzie.

"That's right. I can understand certain words, like *seraphim's song* and a word that means *deity* or *gods*. But it is the meaning or implication of the symbols that I am picking up on rather than just individual words." She continued to study it and after a few moments, "I think it is a code that combines math and music in order to make it possible for humans to communicate with the gods." She looked at the others, "Lyuba called it a 'key' and that is what it is. It's a key that opens a portal between earth and heaven using a specific vibration or tone."

"B flat minor," said Jennifer.

Dara nodded. "And I think it originally came from a place other than Earth. The structure of the crystal is more compressed and more clear than what is found on this planet."

At first no one said anything. They were too stunned. But because the females of intellectual genius had unique ways of deciphering the world's problems as well as their own, and because Carolina was the daughter of a *choov-ihni* with her own special abilities, they all had questions. Questions that were obvious—*Where did it come from?*—*How on earth did it get here?*—*How are we supposed to return it, or even know where to return it?*—*What is its purpose?*

And some questions that were not so obvious and more difficult to say out loud—*Is it dangerous?*—*What will happen to us if we can't return it?*—*What if we are wrong?* And the most frightening question of all—*What does Milosh have to do with it?*

Thousands of miles away from Wood Rose Orphanage and Academy for Young Women, across oceans and continents, Lyuba sat at her table in her hut reading the Tarot and concentrating on the crystal. She knew her daughter and the three young women were looking at the cylinder and trying to understand. Lyuba closed her eyes and turned her face upwards toward the heavens. What they were dealing with was not just from another time, but from another dimension. There were certain steps to be taken, a process they must follow. She must help them to understand and guide them.

*Return it to the* jinzhi de *cave, my daughter. I will be there with you. It is the place where it began.*

# CHAPTER 14

When Milosh went to his trailer after his run-in with Stanwick, he made the decision that he wouldn't move out until Stanwick physically forced him out, which was highly unlikely. The guy seemed weak and he was old. The last thing the archaeologist would want was some sort of fight or altercation. It would be bad publicity for the project and hurt his efforts in getting more funding.

There was something about that cave, and Milosh wanted to know what it was. All of those stories about some fire-breathing pig dragon had probably been invented centuries ago to protect something valuable hidden inside the cave. To keep people out so they wouldn't find it. Well, he wasn't afraid of any pig dragon, fire-breathing or otherwise, and he sure wasn't afraid of an old man who dug in the dirt for a living. Stanwick had surprised him, showing up like that. He would go back to the cave after dark when he was sure no one would be around. That way he wouldn't have to worry about Stanwick sneaking up on him again.

Milosh flopped down on the bed still covered in yellow dirt left by the dust devil storm. Later, after he had slept, he would go into town to get the herbs he needed and a few tools and a flashlight. Then, when it got dark, he would return to the cave.

Carolina and the F.I.G.s were still looking at Tick's bone when someone knocked on the door. When Carolina opened it, a young woman carrying a note pad and some sort of hand-held recording device pushed her way into the living room. She was followed by a tall, unshaven man with a camera strapped around his neck.

"Good. You are here," she said looking around, then at Carolina. "You are Carolina, right?" and not waiting for an answer, "I am Sue, the lifestyle reporter for *The Observer*, and we are doing a human interest story about Jimmy Bob's dog getting lost during the hurricane and bringing you a bone after the storm." Apparently Hank Pollock, Jimmy Bob's friend, had been talking. She briefly noticed then ignored the three F.I.G.s sitting on the sofa as she surveyed the surroundings. Then her eyes stopped on the table, and the object on the towel. "Oh, there it is," she said motioning to the man with her to take a picture.

"We are in the middle of something here, so you must leave," said Carolina. She moved toward the door to show this assertive reporter and her photographer out, but they didn't move. The photographer took several more pictures.

"My goodness, that is some bone," Sue said, bending down to get a closer look at it. "In fact, that looks like it might have come from the Museum of History." She reached out to pick it up.

"Don't touch that," said Dara. She had seen and heard enough. "You were asked to leave." She stood up then and looked down on this short, irritating woman who apparently had forgotten her manners, if she ever had any.

"Right." The reporter wrote something down on her pad completely dismissing Dara. "What are you planning to do with it?" She turned back to Carolina.

"We will return it to where it belongs," Carolina answered, opening the front door wide.

Sue looked at the open door and motioned to her photographer. On the way out she mumbled to the photographer, "If it were mine, I'd sell it."

After they were gone, Carolina locked the door thinking, *too little, too late.* "We have to return this thing as soon as we can," she said. "Once that story gets out… and those pictures… and if someone recognizes it… " She didn't dare finish her thought.

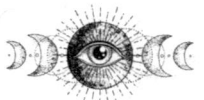

Carolina and the girls worked the rest of the day trying to figure out what sort of device they had, how it worked, what it said, and, most importantly, where it belonged. From what Lyuba had told Carolina, they knew it must have come from the *jinzhi de* cave, and after a little research, they discovered that it was just as Dara suspected. The cave was located in the same area near where Mackenzie's mother had taken them. It was the place where gypsies were believed to have made their home before traveling west into Europe.

"*Jinzhi de* means forbidden," Dara explained. "The Chinese believe that is where the pig dragon lives."

Mackenzie subconsciously touched the birthmark on her shoulder, the mark of a pig dragon and the sign of royalty. It was something she learned when she discovered who her mother was. Before that, it was just a birthmark.

With Jennifer referencing the symphonic poem music she was hearing and the images she was sketching, and Mackenzie interpreting the mathematical equations, algorithms, and whisker chart, and Dara deciphering several more images etched into the crystal, they determined that Tick's bone was coded to react to a certain sound or vibration—specifically, the sound of B flat minor—and when that happened, a portal would open between heaven and earth that would allow communication to take place. "There is a spirituality to it," added Carolina.

In addition, from what Dara was able to decipher from the symbols, the communication included all knowledge from the past, the present, and the future. "The best way to explain it is, it is a compendium of all universal events, thoughts, words, emotions, and intent ever to have occurred in the past, present, or future in terms of all entities and life forms, not just human. Pausing to make sure they understood, she added, "It is like a huge databank."

"By it being removed from the cave, everything has become unbalanced," said Carolina.

"And that might also explain why the seraphim's song is slightly off key," said Jennifer. "Or that scratch on it might have something to do with that."

"It wasn't supposed to be removed from the cave—at least, not yet—and that probably explains the storm," said Mackenzie.

"If that is true, can you imagine the damage to mankind and the horrific destruction that could take place if this doesn't get returned?" said Carolina. "Or if it were to get into the wrong hands?"

All three girls looked at her thinking the same thing. "Milosh!"

They now understood the meaning of Lyuba's message. They knew the seraphim's song, they knew what the key was, and they knew why it had to be protected from evil and returned to where it had come from.

Fearing that if the reporter ran the story it would attract too much attention, some of it possibly being the wrong kind, they decided to make plane reservations leaving Raleigh-Durham International Airport the next day.

With everything set, the F.I.G.s returned to their bungalow to pack, and Carolina called Larry to tell him what they had discovered and what they were planning. She knew he would be upset because he couldn't be there with them to help. "We will only be gone a couple of days," she said, "three at the most," trying to make him feel better. "Just a quick trip to China and back again, so no need to worry at all."

It didn't help.

Not wanting to pack much, Carolina pulled out her small suitcase and her backpack. She would be able to keep both with her on the plane rather than having to check them in. The F.I.G.s were planning to do the same.

The first thing she put into her bag next to Tick's bone wrapped in the green kitchen towel was the *parik-til* Lyuba had made for her when she was a baby. It was something that was included with the other things in the wooden box that had been given to her when she turned eighteen. At the time, she didn't know what it was or its significance. She learned later that it would protect her and always keep her safe, for it came from the *choovihni*—her mother. It had been made just for her.

As she was deciding what else to take, there was a knock on the door. She immediately thought of the reporter. "This really is too much," she said, opening the door. It was Jimmy Bob and Tick.

"Is everything all right, Jimmy Bob?" She bent down smiling and patted Tick on his head. "Such a good boy."

"Ms. Lovel, I am sorry to bother you, but do you have your television on?"

Carolina hadn't turned on the television all day. When she did now, a weather map filled the screen showing a massive storm out in the Atlantic Ocean. She turned up the sound. *Already a category 4, it is expected to make landfall somewhere on the east coast between Virginia Beach and Miami sometime tomorrow. All international flights have been cancelled.* Carolina looked at Jimmy Bob. "Oh my gosh!"

"There's more," he said, pointing to the television.

She turned her attention back to the reporter. *In another part of the world, a magnitude 9 earthquake, the strongest measure on the Richter Scale, has hit Mumbai, the largest city in India located in the territory of Maharashtra. It is unknown at this time how many people have been killed or injured, but early reports show major significant damage.*

*It is being reported from our Australian affiliate that numerous wildfires have broken out across Western Australia and are now threatening Perth, Australia's largest city,* continued the reporter. *Thousands of acres have been destroyed. Authorities are uncertain as to how the fires started, although there is speculation that lightning was the cause.*

She turned to another channel. *The Haleakala volcano on the Hawaiian island of Māui, dormant for almost five hundred years, is erupting. People are evacuating to the nearby island of Oahu.*

Then another—*In northeastern Tanzania, close to the Kenyan border, the Kilimanjaro is showing signs of once again becoming active.* All of the networks were talking about the disasters around the world.

*Closer to home, in Washington State, Mount Rainier, which has not erupted in over 500 years and considered the most dangerous volcano in the Cascade Mountain Range, is spewing heated gases and ash.*

Carolina glanced around the room trying to gather her scattered thoughts, trying to stay calm—another major hurricane, an earthquake, out-of-control fires, erupting volcanoes. The international flights had been cancelled.

She thought of the sealed boxes with the word *PRECIOUS* written on them in purple ink and the photograph albums that were neatly stacked in the closet. She looked at the pillows, slip covers, and curtains she had sewn in the colors that she loved—rusty orange, blue, and goldenrod, the beautiful things Miss Alcott had just given her, and the lavender-colored hydrangea she had cut from one of her bushes outside that now was in a blue glass vase on a small table.

*You must hurry. There is little time,* she heard her mother tell her. The *choovihni* was speaking to her, urgently warning her.

"Jimmy Bob, make sure Headmaster Harcourt knows, and warn everyone that they will have to go back to the basement if the storm looks like it will make landfall at the Outer Banks. More than likely, it will follow the same course as Luoli. If that happens, you will need to help Ms. Larson to get set up again."

After Jimmy Bob left, Carolina ran over to the F.I.G.'s bungalow to find them packing. "They have cancelled all international flights out of Raleigh-Durham," she said when they opened the door. "Another hurricane is coming this way."

"Do you think it is because of Tick's bone?" Dara asked.

Carolina nodded. "There has been a major earth-quake in India, and there are wildfires in Australia. The Haleakala volcano on Māui is erupting, and others are threatening to erupt all around the world. Everything is out of balance. We must get the key back to that cave in the Gansu province, but I'm just not sure how we can get there."

"I have an idea," said Mackenzie after a moment, and she reached for her phone. She was immediately put through to her mother, Ling. Mackenzie told her that it was urgent that the four young women go to Puli. Ling didn't question her daughter. "Stay by your phone," she said. "I will call you right back."

As they waited, Jennifer pulled out her charcoals and canvas board, adding more definition and more color, a golden glow beyond the dark swirling images. More was being revealed. Soon it would be complete.

The hum of B flat minor alternated between soft *adagio* and loud *fortissimo*. Overtones were now more melodic but *scherzo*, like the fast third movement of a symphony, except this was one movement—a symphonic poem that told the story of a locked secret library of all things past, present, and future that only one key would open. She wrote the notes she heard without hesitation on her eight-stave paper, dropping the sheets on the floor as she filled each one, oblivious to everyone and everything around her.

Dara's thoughts focused on the 5000-year-old Sanskrit word "akasha." It meant "space." She was familiar with the Akashic Records that referred to the "hidden library" in space, the Book of Secrets. It was a secret hall of records which could be revealed by retreating into the subconscious mind in a deep state of meditation.

Those who were familiar with them believed the records didn't pass judgement or label actions as good or bad; rather, they simply and objectively stated what has been, what is now, and what will be. Because they were a higher dimension from the dimension currently known to man, the rules of time didn't apply. Rather, time was like a flat circle.

Somehow all of this was connected to Tick's bone.

Carolina sat with Mackenzie, knowing she was frightened, holding her hand. When the phone rang, Mackenzie simply stared at it. Carolina handed it to her. It was Ling.

"Be at Raleigh-Durham International Airport in an hour," she instructed. "Someone will be there to meet you and take you to a private plane. It will fly west and, therefore, avoid the approaching storm coming from the east. Your plane will refuel in Salt Lake City and again in Honolulu before landing at the Jinan Yaoqiang Airport.

"It is a fourteen-hour flight," she explained. "Li Lee, my attaché, is already in Puli doing some work for me at the Yellow Sea Laboratory. He will meet you at the airport to help get you through customs." She sensed Mackenzie's anxiety. "He will take care of everything," she said, "and, please, you must stay at the *zhuang yuan* for as long as you like." The *zhuang yuan* was Ling's family estate where they had stayed before, and Mackenzie wondered if Su Wing would be there. As though reading her thoughts, Ling said, "Su Wing will have everything prepared for you." Su

Wing's family had worked with Ling's family and on the estate for generations. In fact, it was Su Wing's grandfather who made the dandelion pin that Ling had given Mackenzie the first time they met. It symbolized immortality.

"Thank you, Ling." After a slight pause, Mackenzie managed to say, "Mother." The fact that Ling was Mackenzie's mother was still fresh and unfamiliar, and she was not yet comfortable calling this Chinese woman who was a U.S. Senator from Hawaii "mother." But that was all right. Ling understood. It would come in time.

Ling had so many questions—and concerns—for Mackenzie and her friends. But this wasn't the time to ask for answers. That must come later, if and when Mackenzie wanted to let her know. She couldn't be with Mackenzie after she was born or when she was growing up. Only in the background. But that had all changed; she was here now. These young women needed her help, and no matter the reason or the cost, she would provide that help. "Be careful, Mackenzie. Know that all of you will be in my thoughts and that I love you."

After Ling hung up the phone, she silently prayed that the mark of the ancient dragon on Mackenzie's shoulder, the birthmark she had been born with, would protect her. In Chinese culture, the five-clawed coiled yellow dragon with an elongated head that resembled a boar was seen as a symbol of imperial power, a mark of distinction and royalty. Anyone born with the mark was a descendant of Emperor Huangdi who according to legend was immortalized into a dragon and had ascended to Heaven. Because she had been born with it, Mackenzie had the power to rule her own dynasty; she could control her own destiny.

# CHAPTER 15

Milosh waited an extra hour after dark just in case Stanwick decided to return to the site. When he felt all was safe and no one was still working, he returned to the cave carrying the trowel and flashlight he had purchased earlier. Once again he searched the area where he had found the large, heavy artifact hoping to find another, but he found nothing. Disappointed, he made his way deeper into the cave, and when he did the sound of the wind became more noticeable. A low vibrating hum almost like a chant, he found it irritating. There had to be another entrance to the cave and that was what was causing the sound, but he would search for it another time.

Slowly he inched his way through the darkness, stopping to dig where it looked promising. As he had before, he found numerous pieces of broken pottery, but now he was also finding pieces of porcelain. Perhaps the Chinese and gypsies had both lived in the cave either together or separately at different times. In one small area, he found a circle that had been formed by rocks. It looked like a place to burn wood, perhaps a place to cook. The way the rocks had been stacked and arranged in a certain pattern provided more proof that gypsies had once inhabited the cave.

He was just about ready to give up and go back when he noticed just a little farther ahead, the path he was on split into two, leading off in different directions. He followed the path to the left and found on the walls ancient drawings of things that were unidentifiable. They could have been people, he reasoned, but they were very strange, and certainly not from this planet. In other petroglyphs he had seen, the drawings had always been of animals—cows, horses, lions, deer, even antelope—animals that were recognizable. But here in this cave, there was nothing recognizable about the drawings.

There were other paintings in addition to what might be people wearing strange clothing or spacesuits—things that looked like machinery or perhaps vehicles of some sort. He remembered Lyuba teaching the young people in the tribe about vimanas or flying machines that came down from the heavens and visited the people on earth as they were described in the ancient Vedic texts of Sanskrit. Were these petroglyphs what had attracted the gypsies all those centuries ago?

It would soon be light and he had to stop his search. He left the same way he had come, carrying his trowel and flashlight, and his bag of artifacts slung over his shoulder. He would return the next night and explore the other path that went to the right. He was getting close to finding something important, he felt certain. And it was something that would bring to him much wealth.

When he got to the trailer, before doing anything else, he opened the various small packages wrapped in white paper and held together with twine. The shop owner had given him a hard time and had asked him what he planned to do with the poisonous herbs. Milosh told him he had a rat problem. The shop owner sold him the herbs, but Milosh knew he didn't believe his story about rats.

Milosh dumped the poisonous herbs he had purchased into the small glass jar and shook it. Satisfied, he sat on the bed and glanced through an American newspaper which he had also purchased. On page 3 was a short article that had been picked up by the wire services about a dog in Raleigh, North Carolina, getting lost during a major category 5 hurricane named Luoli and finding his way home with a bone. Along with the article was a picture of some young women with a strange object that was presumably the bone. Milosh recognized it immediately. It was the artifact he had found in the cave. The big one that went missing during the dust devil storm.

He read the story again and this time looked more closely at the picture. It was those same three women who had come into the *Kaulo Camio* camp to find the *choovihni* and ask her for help. It was when he had put the curse on the *choovihni's* daughter. "We will return it to where it belongs," the woman named Carolina Lovel was quoted in the article. He recognized the name. Carolina Lovel was the *choovihni's* daughter.

Angrily, Milosh threw the paper, scattering the pages across a table, only to pick it up moments later and read the article again. The *choovihni's* daughter was coming to the *jinzhi de* cave. He grabbed the jar and shook it violently, then tossed it on the floor. The artifact had to be valuable, otherwise why would a reporter write about it for the newspaper? He would be ready. The artifact was his and he would get it back.

When the sun slowly lifted over the horizon, its first bright rays filtered through a dirty window. There in the darkened room Milosh slept soundly on a bed covered in yellow grit in the trailer that had been battered and pit-marked by the *shāchén*. The glass jar, now fogged from its poisonous contents, was on the floor next to the bed.

Carolina and the F.I.G.s stood huddled together in the large concourse of the empty airport. Other than an employee pushing a cleaning mop and emptying trash containers into a large bin, there was no one else around. Before leaving Wood Rose, Carolina had stopped by to tell Mrs. Ball and Miss Alcott that she and the F.I.G.s needed to make a quick trip to China and not to worry. They would inform the headmaster. She also told Jimmy Bob, knowing he would also be concerned.

With everything happening so fast, there had been no time for Carolina to call Larry back to tell him of their change of plans before they left Wood Rose. She tried now knowing he was probably already in class and left him a message when he didn't answer. She had a headache and had taken an aspirin earlier, but it hadn't done any good. And she felt tired. It was more than likely from all of the anxiety and stress.

Not knowing anything other than what Ling had said—to be at the airport in an hour—the young women didn't know what to do. When they heard a door slam at the other end of the concourse, they turned and saw a man rushing towards them. He was in a pilot's uniform.

"I hope you haven't been waiting long," he said apologetically. I am your co-pilot, Bruce Evans. The pilot, Jim Barnes, is already on board going through pre-flight. If you would, please follow me. I will help get you settled and we should be ready for take-off in just a few minutes."

Shortly after boarding and meeting the pilot, the plane was given clearance. Dark ominous clouds were already forming in the east along with intermittent bands of showers. Within minutes, the small jet Boeing Dreamliner lifted off and headed west toward Salt Lake City where it would make the first fuel stop.

There were no other passengers, and the young women spread out—at first. It wasn't long, however, that Mackenzie, then Jennifer, and finally Dara moved to the empty seats next to Carolina. Being alone, even in a seat across the aisle, just wouldn't do. They needed to be close so they could share their thoughts and ideas, their fears, their "what ifs."

Throughout the flight, Jim kept the four young women informed about the storm, giving them updates as he received them from the National Weather Service. It was already a category 4 and, taking the same path as Luoli had, it was headed for the Outer Banks in North Carolina.

Carolina leaned her seat back and closed her eyes. Her head was starting to throb. The F.I.G.s knew Carolina wasn't feeling well, just like before when Milosh put a curse on her and they found Lyuba to help her. Only this time, they couldn't go to Lyuba because she wasn't nearby, and they didn't know what to do.

Carolina was their family, like an older sister. She was one of them. If anything happened to her—Mackenzie reached over and held Carolina's hand. Jennifer shifted in her seat, folding her arms and squeezing tight, trying to ease the pain she felt in her chest; until the large stone got smaller again. Dara stared at the seat in front of her, thinking of words and symbols that she didn't understand except that they resembled an ancient language unknown to man—and they came from another world.

Unlike before, when everyone for the most part cooperated and things went relatively smoothly in preparation for the hurricane at Wood Rose Orphanage and Academy for Young Women, nothing seemed to be working as it should in getting ready for this second hurricane named Michael which, according to the National Weather Service, was taking the same course as Luoli had taken. Even bigger in mass than Luoli, with record-breaking wind speeds over those that had been recorded for Luoli, there had been little warning and even less time to make preparations.

Jimmy Bob with the help of some of the professors managed to pull the cots back out from storage and set them up again, but there wasn't time to neatly line them up against walls in designated, hierarchical, well-organized areas of the safe room as they had been before. Therefore everyone just grabbed a cot and dragged it to wherever they wanted to be.

With no time to replenish supplies and snacks, Ms. Larkins had nothing to put on the one long table moved against the wall other than bottles of water. And although she put out the board games and decks of cards, she hadn't been able to find all of the pieces to the games or cards to the decks from before.

Mrs. Ball and Miss Alcott, already worried to distraction because Carolina and the F.I.G.s had left for China, got into a huff when one of the newly hired professors took one of the large comfortable recliners for himself. This thoughtless, selfish action, however, was quickly remedied when he relinquished it to Miss Alcott after she again threatened him with unemployment, loss of perks, as well as bodily harm. With Jimmy Bob's help, she was soon parked next to her friend, Mrs. Ball, who had full control of the other recliner.

Neither woman, however, could relax. The entire incident with the recliner had upset their already frayed nerves. It didn't need to be spelled out for them—they knew the sudden trip to China had something to do with that cryptic message Carolina's mother had left for her, and they just wanted Carolina and the F.I.G.s to return to Wood Rose safely.

Not only that, Lilian had noticed that Edna Grace had been unusually quiet ever since giving all of those things to Carolina. It just wasn't like her friend not to be full of chatter, no matter what was going on, and she wondered if it had something to do with the albums of photographs and those sealed boxes that had the word *PRECIOUS* written on them in purple ink. Everyone had secrets, and she wouldn't pry. In time, she hoped her friend would be able to talk about it, and she also hoped it wouldn't be anything too traumatic.

Carol and her kittens were back in their wire kennel, but Jimmy Bob had forgotten to bring the blue towel to drape over the kennel in order to give them privacy and to help keep them from getting nervous. And, this time, there was that hound dog right next to their caged territory. Therefore, Carol felt it necessary to loudly vocalize her complaints of having no privacy and feeling nervous by frequently yowling.

Tick, who had been missing during Luoli and, therefore, unfamiliar with the safe room, was relegated to a small area on the bare floor next to the kennel just beyond Carol's clawed pawed reach and the irritating gymnastic antics of one of her kittens—the little black female with the white mark on her forehead in the shape of a pentagram—the mark of the pentacle of Solomon. Apparently Tick wasn't too pleased about the location any more than Carol was because he wouldn't stop whining.

The student-residents—the younger orphans—were still tired from the previous storm, and having had no sleep or very little, they were fussy and loud and looking for trouble. The older student-residents were only too happy to help them find the trouble they were looking for by making teasing remarks and suggestions.

The auxiliary power in the form of a generator that had worked so adequately before, now only sputtered when the lights went out. Jimmy Bob hadn't had time to get more gasoline for it in order to keep it running.

The one positive thing, however, was that Headmaster Thurgood Harcourt hadn't taken the time to unpack the numerous boxes that held all of Wood Rose's important papers, computer discs, and irreplaceable documents as well as the insurance papers from before, and they were stacked neatly next to the cot where he sat watching everyone else.

That is, until the lights went out.

# CHAPTER 16

In the cemetery, Lyuba knelt next to the ancient tree. As the light of day turned to dusk, Lyuba began preparing a mixture using the flowers and herbs—bloodroot, delphinium, oleander, and bishop's weed—what she had collected earlier, and a white powder. To the mixture she added seven drops of water from the nearby creek gently stirring it into a paste. She then placed a lighted black candle into the paste, closed her eyes, and began chanting:

*Milosh,*
*For the pain you have caused me, this revenge is upon you.*
*For the pain you have caused this world and worlds beyond, this revenge is upon you.*
*To you, since my malice has awakened, revenge I have called.*
*To you, who have dragged me to hatred, revenge I have called.*
*May your destiny be forever changed.*
*Your own evil now returns to you.*
*You no longer will have the pleasure of doing harm.*
*A curse that will last a hundred years.*
*May the earth devour you.*
*So be it.*

It was done. Lyuba blew out the candle.

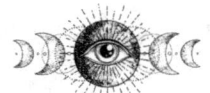

Milosh awoke just before sunrise. He had meant to get up earlier. It angered him now that he must rush. Putting on the same dirty clothes he had worn the day before, he ran to the cave not taking time to eat anything. He needed to get there before any of the others arrived so he wouldn't be seen.

The story in the newspaper had quoted the *choovihni's* daughter saying, "We will return it to where it belongs." She had used the word "we" which meant those other three girls would probably be with her. It didn't matter. As long as he got rid of the one named Carolina. Lyuba would regret not showing him respect.

He left the trailer in such a hurry, he forgot to shake the jar, not remembering until he had already reached the site. He would do it later, after he finished exploring in the cave. He wanted to see what he could find on that other path, and, if he had time, figure out where the wind was coming from.

It was almost light when he got to the dig site; no one else was around. He quickly entered the cave. The sound of the wind was even stronger than it had been the day before, and he could hear it closer to the entrance of the cave. A steady vibrating hum was so loud that loose rocks started to fall around him, keeping him distracted and making it difficult to walk as he tried to avoid twisting an ankle or being hit. He didn't stop to explore until he got to where the path split into two, this time taking the path going to the right to see if there was anything of interest.

He planned to spend the day in the cave, not knowing when she would arrive. If she didn't come that day, he would return the next day, and the day after that. However long it took. He would wait for the *choovihni's* daughter. He would get what was rightfully his.

It wasn't long before Milosh could hear noises and people talking outside the cave. The others working the site had arrived, and they were all talking about the natural disasters that were occurring around the world. Dr. Stanwick usually brought something for them to eat before they started to work, and Milosh was starting to get hungry. He should have gotten up earlier so he could eat something.

He examined the walls of this new path and found even more ancient cave drawings similar to what he had seen on the previous day. These drawings, however, appeared to be even older. Stick figures with humanoid and animal characteristics, and more of the shapes that looked like vehicles, but it was impossible to be sure what they were since he had never seen anything like them before.

And then, ahead of him on the stone wall, illuminated by his flashlight, he saw it.

It was a painted picture, ancient—massive and detailed, with the rich primary colors of blue, red, yellow, and green made from plant pigments and animal secretions, things found in nature, of what looked like the heavens, the entire solar system, with stars and planets and galaxies, the constellations. It was all there, etched in color on the flat surface of an enormous flat stone wall. It was perfect. It had been untouched and probably unseen for millennia—maybe since the beginning of time.

What caught his eye, however, was in the middle of all of the heavenly cosmos detail was a picture of what appeared to be the big artifact with the carved symbols he had found. It was painted in gold. It had to be significant, its value even greater than he had first imagined. This had to be the reason why the early gypsies had settled here in this place.

He sat down in front of the large petroglyph, studying it for clues as to what it meant. Somehow it was all connected—this picture of the universe and the artifact he had found wedged in the cave wall.

He would be patient. He would watch and wait for the *choovihni's* daughter to return the artifact to the cave. He couldn't risk someone else getting to it before he did, and he knew Stanwick was ready to go into the cave, even if he had to go in alone. Milosh would come back the next day and the next if necessary—except the next time he would bring something to eat.

Everything was working out even better than he had imagined. He would get his revenge on Lyuba for having him banned from his tribe and disowned by his family. For disrespecting him. This time he had put a powerful curse on her daughter that even the *choovihni* wouldn't be able to reverse. And he would soon have all the riches he ever wanted because he had found an artifact worth more than rubies. Its value was so great it couldn't even be determined. It was an artifact that he knew men would kill for.

When they finally arrived at the Jinan Yaoqiang Airport, Jim gave Carolina and the F.I.G.s a phone number for them to call when they were ready to return to Raleigh. "This is where we will be," he said. "The Senator instructed us to stay until you were ready to leave."

Bruce added, "When you are ready to leave, or if you need anything before then, just call that number."

The Jinan Yaoqiang Airport was just as they had remembered from the first time they traveled to this part of the world. Being in one of the busiest airports in China, in the country with the largest population in the world, they pushed their way through the throngs of chattering people. As before, everyone, it seemed, was moving in a different direction.

The modern dramatic architectural element of the enormous walls of glass, the many signs in English, and the large black arrows pointing to customs were now familiar to them. They didn't try to talk, knowing they wouldn't be heard over all of the clamor and confusion. They simply struggled to keep up with one another, Carolina most of all. Feverish, she felt weak and had difficulty walking, her headache was much worse, and her hearing was becoming distorted—fuzzy. What Carolina did hear, however, was Lyuba's voice. *I am here with you, my daughter. Go to the cave and I will be there.*

When they finally made their way through all of the dizzying noise and chaos and arrived at customs, they were relieved to see Li Lee, Senator Yi's attaché, waiting for them. He smiled and waved. The well-dressed, soft-spoken man, small in stature, extremely polite, and totally efficient would take care of everything, Ling had said. Just as he did before when they came to China, after showing his credentials to authorities, he collected their luggage and escorted the young women through the madness of customs without any delay to the car outside.

The comfort and quiet of the car was more than welcomed given the fact that they had been on a plane for better than fourteen hours. Putting the airport behind them, they drove out of the city into the green, mountainous countryside. If Li Lee was surprised when Carolina asked him to take them to where the Luoli Archaeological Project was located near the *jinzhi de* cave and the Yellow Sea in the Gansu province, he didn't show it. He was more concerned over her appearance. She didn't look well. Pale and somewhat listless, he worried that the trip had been too much for her. He made polite conversation when they wanted to talk, but he didn't ask any questions as to the purpose of their visit. And when they grew quiet, he let them rest.

It was early morning when they arrived at the cave, and there were several people already at work, digging in different areas that were identified by roped grids near the entrance to a cave. Dara, Mackenzie, and Jennifer followed Carolina, instinctively knowing, just as Tick knew, this was something she had to do. They could only be there to help her as females of intellectual genius; the actual physical act of returning the key to where it belonged had to be accomplished by Carolina.

*Go to the man with white hair,* Carolina heard her mother say. *He will understand. He will help you.*

# ChAPTER 17

With only candles, a few flashlights, and the illumination from phones to provide light, most of the safe room in the dormitory basement was relatively dark. Rather than stumbling around and bumping into things, everyone stayed put for the most part. At one point someone—it sounded like Professor Sullivan—asked where Carolina and the F.I.G.s were, but no one answered. Mrs. Lilian Ball and Miss Edna Grace Alcott knew, of course, as did Jimmy Bob, but in their opinion it was no one's business, including Headmaster Harcourt's, unless he specifically asked. Therefore, they kept that information to themselves.

This storm was even worse than Luoli had been, and it was more terrifying. Sounds of glass shattering somewhere upstairs, crunching, screeching banging noises of wood against wood and metal against metal, loud thumps that shook the entire stone structure, the cracking splintering noise of trees breaking and falling to the ground, and the most terrifying of all, the sounds that couldn't be identified. Unable to do anything else, the orphans, faculty, and staff of Wood Rose remained in the safe room, waiting anxiously and hoping the storm would soon pass and things could go back to being as they should.

Larry immediately checked his phone again for messages from Carolina as soon as he got out of class. If she and the F.I.G.s left early like she said in her previous message, they would already have landed. They were twelve hours ahead of the local time in Buenos Aires. He tried calling her, but she didn't answer. He checked the national weather app on his phone, and it showed North Carolina, getting hammered by Hurricane Michael. All projections showed the storm moving inland on the same path Hurricane Luoli had taken—directly toward Raleigh.

There were also warnings about a line of severe weather in Bahia Blanco just 574 kilometers away heading northeast toward Buenos Aires. They were under a tornado alert. More than likely classes would have to be cancelled.

Switching to the news update app, everything he read had to do with the natural disasters happening all around the globe. When he looked up current weather conditions in Puli, China, it showed there had been a major earthquake 100 miles to the east of that city. Vibrations could be felt as far west as the Yellow Sea in the Gansu province. That was where Carolina and the F.I.G.s were headed.

Carolina had told him about the safe room at Wood Rose where everyone had gone during Luoli. Now with Michael having already made landfall on the Outer Banks and moving west at a rapid speed toward Raleigh, more than likely the basement of the dormitory was where everyone would be.

He had the telephone numbers for three people at Wood Rose he felt were responsible and who cared for the wellbeing of Carolina and the females of intellectual genius. Any one of these people he could call in case of emergency—Mrs. Lilian Ball, Miss Edna Grace Alcott, and Jimmy Bob Doake—that is, if he could even get through. If everyone was evacuated to the basement, he doubted if there would be phone service.

He tried the number for Mrs. Ball first. If anyone had information about Carolina and the F.I.G.s, assuming he could get through, it would be Lilian Ball.

Dr. Stanwick was examining some recent finds spread out on the table when he noticed a black car drive up and park. Four young women got out of the car and walked toward where he was working. Each woman was carrying a backpack. At first he thought they were perhaps tourists just visiting the site, but seeing their faces as they approached, he knew it was something more serious.

Carolina offered her hand to introduce herself, and then the F.I.G.s. Dr. Stanwick recognized the name of one of the young women. Dara Roux was the person his friend and colleague, Dr. Wu, was bringing to visit the site in a few weeks, but before he could say anything, Carolina opened her backpack and pulled out something wrapped in a green towel. When she uncovered it, Dr. Stanwick gasped and grabbed the edge of the table. He immediately knew.

"Where did you get this?" he asked, barely able to speak. Carefully, he removed it from the towel and began examining it. It was even more magnificent than he had imagined. To have dreamed of seeing it since childhood, to have searched for it most of his entire adult life, and now actually holding it was almost overwhelming. Very few things in his life had meant so much to him, and had brought him to tears. This, however, was one such moment.

Everything about it was perfect: its form and balance, the clarity and density of the crystal, the sharpness of the etchings. It was beautiful. Man could not have made such an object. It had to come from the gods.

Over the next several minutes, Carolina and the three females of intellectual genius tried to explain something that couldn't be explained—the curse, Milosh, the hurricane, Lyuba, Wood Rose, Tick. And then, in more detail—an ancient language that was pre-Sumerian, similar to Sanskrit and ancient Egyptian hieroglyphs, yet from an earlier time still and maybe even before any known civilizations and possibly from another world—another dimension; elements between music, such as its form, rhythm and meter, the pitches of its notes and the tempo of its pulse, to math as it could be related to the measurement of time and frequency; and a single continuous musical composition—the symphonic poem that was evoking through music the content of something non-musical, such as an ancient artifact.

None of these things, either singular or together, made any sense. Yet, because Dr. Stanwick remembered the stories from his childhood and held them close, because he believed that places and things thought to be based on myth, legend, and fantasy were actually based on reality, and because he was an archaeologist with a passion for preserving the past for the future over personal recognition and glory, he understood. He trusted these four young women who had flown so far to accomplish something so urgent not just for themselves, but for all of humanity. He believed them. He also now understood the reason Milosh had wanted so desperately to work at the archaeological dig site; specifically, the Luoli Project.

Lyuba had not slept. She gazed into the crystal ball and saw the small glass jar discarded haphazardly onto the floor; what it was holding, hidden. Through the fogged glass, she eventually saw the inside of the jar, and when she had identified its contents, she knew what Milosh had done. Her precious daughter wouldn't be able to fight the curse. She would die. She would die in the *jinzhi de* cave.

Knowing she had very little time, she left her hut and once again returned to the large aged tree in the cemetery. There was only one thing she could do. Kneeling there under the low spreading limbs that had survived centuries of storms, droughts, disease, and battles between men, she presented her offering. Made in unconditional love and without hesitation, it was an offering of the life of a *choovihni* in exchange for the life of the *choovihni's* daughter.

She pleaded to the gods, to all that was, all that is, and all that is still to come. She bowed her head in humble reverence, in submission, presenting herself—a gypsy *choovihni*—born with the knowledge of life and healing as it had been passed down to her by her mother, and her mother's mother, and generations before. Then lying on the ground beneath the tree, her eyes closed, she outstretched her arms. She was giving all she had to offer—herself. She had nothing more to give.

The air around her grew still and motionless—expectant. Lyuba did not breathe.

Droplets of rain started to fall from the sky—cleansing and pure. Lyuba did not move.

A gentle breeze blew against her body—caressing her, drying her. Lyuba thought of her daughter, imploring the gods to watch over her, protect her, and keep her safe.

Moments passed, meaningful and deep.

She heard a fluttering sound coming from the tree, and when she opened her eyes, above her, she saw the single magpie; then several. And then, suddenly, scores of black magpies darkened the sky and settled on the large low hanging branches and all of the many smaller branches above them. A good sign.

Once they were settled and quiet, two owls came and landed on the uppermost branch closest to the heavens and to the gods that dwelled therein. Another good sign.

When the brightness of the sun pierced through the leaves and warmed its many branches, the ancient tree and everything around it radiated in a brilliant golden light, and it was then that Lyuba knew. She had been heard. The gods had answered.

Her daughter would be saved.

The *choovihni* would continue to live.

Gathering herself up from the ground, Lyuba once again knelt and gave worshipful thanks to the tree and to the gods. She had been blessed.

When she left the cemetery, she returned to her hut, for there was much more to be done. Carolina still needed her help. Lyuba would read the Tarot and gaze into the crystal. She would find the answers.

# CHAPTER 18

When Li Lee watched the four young women follow the white-haired gentleman into the cave with nothing but their backpacks and flashlights, he grew concerned. The Senator had told him to call if there were any problems using her private number in Washington, D.C., where she would be. After waiting a few minutes, and feeling increasingly uncomfortable when Carolina and the F.I.G.s didn't reappear, he took out his phone and dialed the number that would reach U.S. Senator Xing-Ling Yi from Hawaii directly.

As though expecting his call, she answered immediately. Of course she was familiar with the *jinzhi de* cave. She had taken the four young women to visit the area near the cave when they had travelled to China before. It was the fact that many archaeologists and anthropologists believed it to be the earliest home for the gypsies, even before they started to settle throughout Europe, she thought would interest them. And it had.

But why was it so urgent that they return now? With air travel almost impossible because of so much danger and the many threats of disaster around the globe, what could be the reason that they needed to return to the *jinzhi de* cave—now?

At a very early age, Ling had learned of the ancient pig dragon. She had been taught well by her father who was head of the ruling family of Qiang. She knew that those who disrespected it would suffer. Those who believed in it would not be threatened or harmed by it. But those who understood it carried its mark—the mark of the pig dragon, for they were royalty. It was the mark of greatness. Ling's grandmother had the mark, as did her mother. That mark had been passed down to Ling. And now her daughter, Mackenzie, bore the mark. Was that the reason they needed to go to the cave? Was the pig dragon summoning Mackenzie for some reason?

Ling's questions caused her to be deeply afraid for her daughter. She touched the mark of the pig dragon on her shoulder, the same mark that was on her daughter's shoulder. "Stay close to them, Li Lee," she told her personal attaché, "and keep watch. They might be in danger and not realize it."

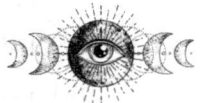

As Larry suspected, all classes were suspended until further notice. The Dean of the Philosophy Department told him he would get back in touch with him later and set up another time—perhaps during spring semester—for him to return to Buenos Aires and teach the classes on ancient Asian philosophy. It had been a popular course, and the students had particularly enjoyed his lectures on Confucius and his teachings on man being the best he could be, Sun Tzu, a military genius who advised kings, and Lao Tzu, a natural free spirit, the Dean told him.

After several attempts to reach Mrs. Ball with no success, Larry was starting to become seriously worried about what was happening to Carolina and the F.I.G.s. He needed to go home to Wood Rose. He spent the next thirty minutes trying to find a flight that would take him to North Carolina. But because of the storm, nothing was flying, not even private planes.

Unable to get a flight out of Buenos Aires, he did the only thing he could do. He called the nearest car rental place that was conveniently located within walking distance from the Universidad de Buenos Aires and rented a car. He would drive back to Raleigh. It was at least 5000 miles, but he could drive all night and only stop to rest and grab something to eat when he absolutely had to. That way, at least he would be there when they returned—if they could return.

While waiting at the car rental place for the car to be brought around, he called his friend Grai in New York City. With only one name, meaning "horse" in Romani, Grai was Larry's best friend. He and Larry had grown up together. They were from the same tribe of travelers and had been taught by the same *choovihni*. Through the years they had remained in frequent contact.

Just as Larry did, Grai also decided at a young age to leave the gypsy ways for another life and a different culture, and when he was old enough he moved to New York where he attended New York University. His undergraduate degree was in public service, and he later graduated from law school. Now he owned his own taxi which he drove part-time in New York City, and he lived at Mrs. Gertrude Killebrew's boarding house where he did odd jobs and repair work for her in addition to being her security guard. In exchange, he had a nice comfortable place to live and good food to eat. Grai was a decent, honest man, he was smart, and he had the instincts of a gypsy. Larry trusted him.

When Carolina and the F.I.G.s went to New York City in search of Dara's mother, Larry arranged for them to stay at Mrs. Killebrew's who had been operating her boarding house for over thirty years. It was a place he was familiar with since it was where he stayed whenever he went to New York to visit Grai. "When her husband passed on, she decided she wanted to keep doing what she loved," Larry told Carolina, and that was to keep running her boarding house. Of course, without her husband there to help her, she had to hire a couple of people, Grai being one of them, and Mrs. Rothstern, a strong, middle-aged woman who came in on Wednesdays and did all of the cleaning. "Mrs. Killebrew is a little bit crusty, but her bark is worse than her bite. Hers is an older home and it isn't anything fancy, but it is clean and the food is good. I think you and the F.I.G.s will like it," Larry had reassured her. He also knew that his friend Grai would be there to look after the young women.

Larry was right. Carolina and the F.I.G.s had loved it from the moment they saw the brick two-story house with a dark gray shingled roof, one of several on a narrow tree-lined street. Beds of zinnias growing in abundance along the front of the house and flanking the wide stone steps leading up to the porch made them feel welcomed, as did the large hand-painted wooden sign letting them know that they had arrived at *Mrs. Killebrew's Boarding House.*

And they loved Mrs. Killebrew, even with her sharp tongue. She had a kind heart and a generous spirit which was made evident by the fresh flowers—zinnias—she placed in their rooms each day, and making sure they always had a good meal to eat even when they violated house rules by being late. It was Mrs. Killebrew and the comfort of her beautiful old home that they knew they could return to at the end of each day after experiencing untold danger, tremendous anxiety, and the heart-breaking disappointment that came with trying to find Dara's mother.

Grai had taken them wherever they needed to go. It was also Grai who had almost lost his own life in order to save their lives in a secret area inhabited by what could only be described as a sub-culture beneath the tracks of Grand Central Terminal. Larry would never forget what he had done.

Grai picked up on the third ring; he sounded like he was at the bottom of a well.

"My friend! ¡Hola! How is Buenos Aires? And how are Carolina and the F.I.G.s?"

"Classes have been suspended because of tornadoes in the area," answered Larry, "and Carolina and the F.I.G.s are either on their way to China or they are already there. Where are you? You sound strange."

Grai laughed. "I am under the kitchen sink fixing a leak for Mrs. Killebrew. She is really excited about seeing all of you over Thanksgiving again. She has me working day and night trying to get everything ready. You ought to see her list." Then, realizing what Larry just said, "China?"

"Actually, that is the reason I am calling." Larry glanced around to make sure no one could overhear his conversation and lowered his voice. "When we were being instructed by the *choovihni*, do you remember learning anything about a special key or something called the seraphim's song?"

"Hold on." Larry heard Grai grunt and the sound of metal dropping on a hard surface—probably a wrench—and a scooting sound; he was getting out from under the sink.

"That was a long time ago. We weren't very old. Let me think for a moment. The *choovihni* used the word *key* for a lot of symbolism, if I remember correctly. But the seraphim's song…

"Wait a minute. I think I do remember now. It was when she was teaching us the early history of gypsies—about the first Romani. In the beginning where the first-known gypsies came into being there was a key with a code that could open a portal and allow man to communicate with the gods. But it could only happen if the right vibration or sound occurred at the same time, and that was the song of the seraphim."

Larry remembered. Hearing Grai talk about it brought it all back as though it were only yesterday. It was one of the *choovihni's* better stories, and for a while, he and Grai looked everywhere for the key. At ten years of age, what did they know?

Grai laughed. "I think you and I thought we were going to get rich if we found that key. We didn't realize until we got much older that it was in a cave in China." He stopped talking. "Larry? Is that why Carolina and the F.I.G.s are in China?" Then… "Oh no."

Larry told him about the hurricane and Tick and the artifact, and that Lyuba was warning Carolina about Milosh. "Because of Lyuba's warnings, Dara, Mackenzie, and Jennifer think that Milosh somehow had something to do with the artifact showing up in Raleigh, and that is the reason for all of the natural disasters that are happening now all over the world. They believe the artifact is the key."

"Everything is definitely out of balance," said Grai. "And if it is because the key has been taken from the *jinzhi de* cave before it is time for it to be found, things will only get worse." The heaviness of the situation was unfathomable. The task ahead of Carolina and the F.I.G.s was almost impossible, even without the added complication of a rogue gypsy trying to harm Carolina. "What can I do to help?" asked Grai.

"Nothing right now," and Larry told him about his plan to drive back to Raleigh. "I feel totally helpless, but at least I will be there when they get home." The silence was deafening. Although they didn't say it, both men were thinking the same thing—*If they get home.*

As soon as he hung up, Mrs. Killebrew came bustling into the kitchen with her list. She had added some things to it that she needed to discuss with Grai. When she saw Grai's face, however, she forgot her list. "What's wrong?"

she asked. "Can't you fix the leak?"

"The leak is fixed, but I need to take a few days off," he answered.

Mrs. Killebrew knew it had to be something serious. Grai never took any time off. That was why she had learned to rely on him for everything. She pulled out a kitchen chair and sat in it. "OK, tell me what has happened."

"I think Larry needs me right now," he said.

"Are Carolina and the F.I.G.s all right?" She stood up and pushed her wire-rimmed glasses up from where they had slid down on her nose. It was a gesture that Grai understood well, because it usually meant she was deeply troubled about something.

"As far as I know, but they are in China, and with all of the bad things that have been happening everywhere... " He tried to downplay his fears. The last thing he wanted was to upset or worry Mrs. Killebrew. He knew how much she had grown to love Carolina and the females of intellectual genius. And she had known Larry for as long as she had known him. She considered him as one of her own.

Mrs. Killebrew sat back down and fanned herself with the hem of her apron. Of course she knew he wasn't telling her everything. She could always tell. And she suspected that whatever was going on with Carolina and those three girls was important and probably dangerous. Otherwise Grai wouldn't want to take some time off. He would never leave her alone unless it was something very serious.

"I can arrange for someone to come in while I am away—just to make sure you don't need anything," Grai quickly added. He tried to word it so it wouldn't sound like he thought she was incapable of taking care of herself. It didn't quite work.

"No you will not! I will make it just fine—just like I did when my husband died and before you came along. The only reason I took you in was to keep you off the streets of New York so you wouldn't embarrass yourself."

Of course, Grai knew that wasn't true, and he loved Mrs. Gertrude Killebrew like she was his own mother. All the same, he would ask Mrs. Rothstern to just drop by while he was away.

"Now stop standing around here and getting in my way. You need to pack and get on the road. It's a long drive."

"I will call you once I know more," he told her.

"Well, you'd just better!"

Mrs. Killebrew was sitting in one of the rocking chairs on the front porch when he left. She had packed some sandwiches and freshly baked cookies for him to eat on the way.

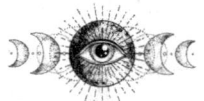

Carolina and her girls followed Dr. Stanwick into the dark cave with the flashlights he provided and their backpacks. They were grateful that he gave them the commercial-grade, heavy duty flashlights to use because the ones they had brought with them would never have been able to penetrate the deep darkness of the cave.

There was a path of sorts, but it was the stone walls of the cave they were most interested in, reasoning that a wall would be the most likely place the artifact would have been hidden. Dr. Stanwick had also told them that the stories about the key he had read as a child growing up always mentioned a stone wall.

Rocks were starting to fall around them, small at first, but getting larger the deeper they went into the cave. Dr. Stanwick noticed disturbed places in the hard clay soil where they walked and on the rock face where Milosh had haphazardly dug, and the destruction he left behind as he violated the walls and floor of the cave. There was no telling what damage he had caused, but this wasn't the time to think about it. He needed to help these young women on a mission that would determine quite possibly whether life would continue on this planet or be completely destroyed.

In hindsight, he wished that he had already explored the cave, even on his own. That way at least he would be familiar with the layout of it. They needed to find some sort of opening or crack in the stone of the wall in which the artifact would fit. Not knowing how deep the cave went, it could take hours of searching. Even days, and they still might not be able to find it.

Carolina was struggling. She had trouble focusing, and she couldn't keep her balance. If anyone spoke, she didn't hear them. The F.I.G.s stayed close to her, holding her arms to steady her, kicking small rocks out of her way so she wouldn't stumble; terrified she was going to die. They wanted desperately to help her, yet they knew the only way they could do that was to find the place where Tick's bone belonged. They needed to return the key.

Mackenzie was the first to see it. About five feet from the ground, the crevasse was the exact same shape and size as the artifact. It had to be where the artifact belonged. The face of the rock around the crevasse was chipped, as though someone had hammered it or dug into it with a sharp tool. Dr. Stanwick placed his hands on the wall, brushing away stone fragments, and gently stroking it as though to repair the damage that had been done and to atone for the thoughtless desecration.

Carolina felt dizzy, and everything around her was spinning uncontrollably. Dropping her backpack to the ground, she had difficulty opening it—she couldn't seem to make the zipper or snap enclosures work—and she could barely breathe. When she finally got it open, she removed the artifact still wrapped in the towel and tried to push it into the crevasse of the stone wall, but it wouldn't go. The opening was too small. "Try it without the towel, Carolina," Dara suggested, forcing herself to stay calm, wanting to do it for her—wanting to shove the thing into the crack—but knowing she couldn't. It had to be Carolina.

Carolina bent down and carefully unwrapped the artifact, then stuffed the towel into her backpack. When she stood up, she glimpsed something—something moving—someone coming towards her from the black depths of the cave.

*Danger is near, daughter, and it is evil.* Carolina heard her mother and tried to see what or who was coming toward her. Her vision was blurred and whatever was moving toward her was obscured by darkness.

She blinked her eyes forcing herself to focus. Then she saw through the darkness. She saw evil.

It was Milosh.

"That is mine," he said, his voice filled with hate and loathing. He lunged at Carolina, trying to grab the artifact, but as he did, Dara screamed at him, "Leave her alone!" When he reached for Carolina again, Dara shoved him causing him to stumble backward and fall, pulling Dara down with him.

Her body trembling, with time running out, Carolina tried to push the artifact into the crevasse, but she was just too weak and disoriented, her vision faded almost to the point of blindness. She couldn't see the opening well enough to fit the artifact into it. She felt the wall and ran her hands over its cool surface, searching for the opening with her fingers. When she found it, the artifact was positioned wrong. It needed to be aligned with the crevasse.

"Push, Carolina!" In desperation, Mackenzie put her hands on top of Carolina's and pushed as hard as she could. Still, it wouldn't slide into the crevasse. "Dara!" Mackenzie yelled. "Help us!"

Dr. Stanwick grabbed Milosh's arm and held on, trying to prevent him from getting up off the ground while Dara squeezed in next to Carolina and put her hands on top of Mackenzie's. Together, Carolina, Mackenzie, and Dara pushed. The stone wall quivered, then the fissure spread open just slightly, and in that one brief second, Tick's bone slipped into the crack.

The artifact fit.

The key had been returned.

Milosh yanked his arm away from Dr. Stanwick's grasp and crawled toward the wall, slipping over the loose stones on the ground when he tried to stand up. Just as he reached for the crevasse, the earth rumbled violently and enormous rocks began falling all around them forming what looked like a cymatic pattern.

A simple circle at first, the earth's vibration caused it to rapidly evolve. It looked like something worshipped by Native Americans and other indigenous people all over the world because they believed it gave them the power to see and understand all things unknown. It looked like a god's eye.

They could hear the vibrating hum of B flat minor, the "aum" sound loud and distinct, clear and pure, no longer off key.

And they could hear the terrifying sound of the stone walls crumbling and the ceiling collapsing from within the inner deep dark depths of the cave and moving closer toward them. Thick choking dust filled the air around them making it almost impossible to breathe or see. "Get out!" shouted Dr. Stanwick. "Run! The cave is collapsing!"

Protecting their heads with their backpacks from the falling rocks, blinded by the thick dust and barely able to breathe, the F.I.G.s ran back the way they had come, toward the entrance, stumbling over broken rocks, pulling Carolina, urging her to hurry, trying to keep her from falling, with Dr. Stanwick right behind them. When they approached the opening of the cave and could see the daylight beyond, Carolina glanced back. The last thing she saw was the crevasse in the stone wall slowly closing around the artifact as though to once again conceal it and protect it. The cymatic pattern of the god's eye was now just a pile of rocks.

Startled by the sudden loud rumble and seeing the thick yellow dust spew from the mouth of the cave, Li Lee quickly got out of the car and rushed toward the noise of falling rocks just as Carolina and the F.I.G.s and Dr. Stanwick exited out of the yellow cloud of darkness and into the bright sunshine. From a safe distance, they watched in stunned silence as huge boulders, uprooted shrubs, small trees, and chunks of yellow clay fell from the outcropping and cliffs above, completely sealing the entrance. Any visible evidence that there was a *jinzhi de* cave or ever had been was gone—destroyed. All that remained was the thick yellow dust slowly rising and dissipating into the air.

"Jennifer!" Dara looked around. "Where's Jennifer?" Dara yelled, moving toward the cave. "Oh, no! Jennifer!"

With everything happening, they hadn't noticed that Jennifer wasn't with them. Running back to the cave's entrance, horrified, Carolina, Dara, and Mackenzie screamed for Jennifer as they clawed and heaved and pushed at the heavy stones in desperation, trying to move them out of the way, trying to get back into the cave—trying to save the female of intellectual genius. Knowing it was futile, Dr. Stanwick fell to the ground, gasping for breath and overcome with emotion. Li Lee knelt beside him, his heart breaking over the tragic hopelessness of it all, knowing there was absolutely nothing they could do.

Through their screams, they heard someone yell, "She's over there." It was one of the workers pointing in the direction of the Yellow Sea.

Jennifer stood on the shoreline motionless, completely lost in her own world of musical notes and painted images as she looked out across the vast expanse of water, her arms wrapped around her canvas board as she held it tightly to her breast. Carolina, Dara, and Mackenzie rushed to her, sobbing and hugging her, unable to control their emotions.

They thought they had lost her; they thought they would never see her again. That would have been like losing a part of themselves, even worse. Losing one female of intellectual genius to death would have been like all of them being lost to death, and it was something for which Carolina would never have been able to forgive herself.

Unable to say anything after reassuring themselves that Jennifer was all right, Carolina and the three females of intellectual genius stood quietly, arms wrapped around each other and Jennifer's painting, allowing the calming effects of the natural untouched beauty of the Yellow Sea soothe them, breathing its cleansing air, trying to accept the truth of what in fact they had accomplished, and to believe that the threat was really no longer present.

"It is so beautiful," Jennifer said, tears running down her cheeks. "In the years to come, we will have many other dangers ahead of us and great mysteries to solve, but we will be able to face them. We are Carolina and the F.I.G.s. That is what is meant to be. *We* are meant to be." Reaching out to Carolina, "You're going to be alright. You aren't going to die."

Jennifer had seen the portal; she had heard the communication from the gods. Her symphonic poem was complete; her painting was finished. The images she first thought were dark ominous clouds with a deadly bolt of lightning were actually the heavens—galaxies immeasurable light years away. And in the center was a golden portal. It was the pathway that allowed the gods in the heavens to communicate with man on earth.

Suddenly remembering, Carolina looked back toward where the cave entrance had been, "Milosh!?"

But he was nowhere to be seen.

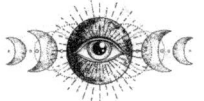

After leaving Dr. Stanwick and the Luoli Project, Li Lee drove the exhausted young women to the *zhuang yuan*—Ling's family estate. He had much to report to the Senator about what he saw and what he heard, but he would do that later in private. Right then, it was important that Carolina and the three F.I.G.s get much-needed rest.

He had called ahead to let Su Wing know they were

on their way, and she was waiting there to greet them. Knowing they must be tired, she showed the four young women to their rooms, the same beautiful rooms they had stayed in before, making them as comfortable as possible and wanting them to feel at home.

Attached to their rooms, they each had a private bath in the sprawling, single-storied home with its beautiful hip-and-gable *irimoya* roof. All were located near one another in one wing of many other wings—like spokes in a wheel—opening onto a brick-paved courtyard with a fountain in the center. The familiarity of Ling's family home was comforting. It gave them the feeling of peace—and, strangely enough, hope.

After they had a chance to rest and freshen up, Su Wing served them in the dining room. Hot pot with mushroom sauce for Carolina, Sichuan pork for Mackenzie, braised pork balls for Dara, Chinese dumplings for Jennifer; she remembered all of their favorite dishes from when they visited before. She was pleased to see Mackenzie wearing the dandelion pin, the beautiful pin Su Wing's grandfather had made and given to Ling when she was a young girl. Now Ling's daughter wore it, and it made her happy. The dandelion symbolized immortality.

Like Li Lee, she asked no questions. She only wished to serve these four special young women who meant so much to Ling.

The earth's shock waves and vibrations of the cave-in had reached as far as the large thicket of forest due north and several kilometers inland of where the *jinzhi de* cave was located. The area, although still rocky, had somewhat of a flat terrain covered in dense tall trees and thick underbrush that was home to the golden pheasant and the Xinjiang ground-jay, tortoises, and various species of frogs and other small wildlife.

Younger trees that still had undeveloped root systems, and dead branches from the larger established trees, had broken or been uprooted by the strong earth tremors and fallen to the ground. Otherwise, there was little evidence of the cataclysm that had occurred a little more than a mile away.

Cave-ins, like the *shāchén* or dust devils, were a frequent occurrence in this region of the ancient Gansu province which bordered the Yellow Sea. They were for the most part ignored as people went about their daily lives. This forest, in particular, although admired for its natural beauty, was left unexplored since there had never been any reason to do otherwise.

Therefore, when the sudden slight depression in the earth appeared deep in the dark woods, it went unobserved, as did the fact that it quickly developed into a small sinkhole revealing the hidden entrance to a cave.

Also unobserved was the young gypsy man with a dark brown *chakra*. Bloodied and caked in thick yellow dust, he painfully crawled his way out of the sinkhole—like evil being unleashed from the gates of hell.

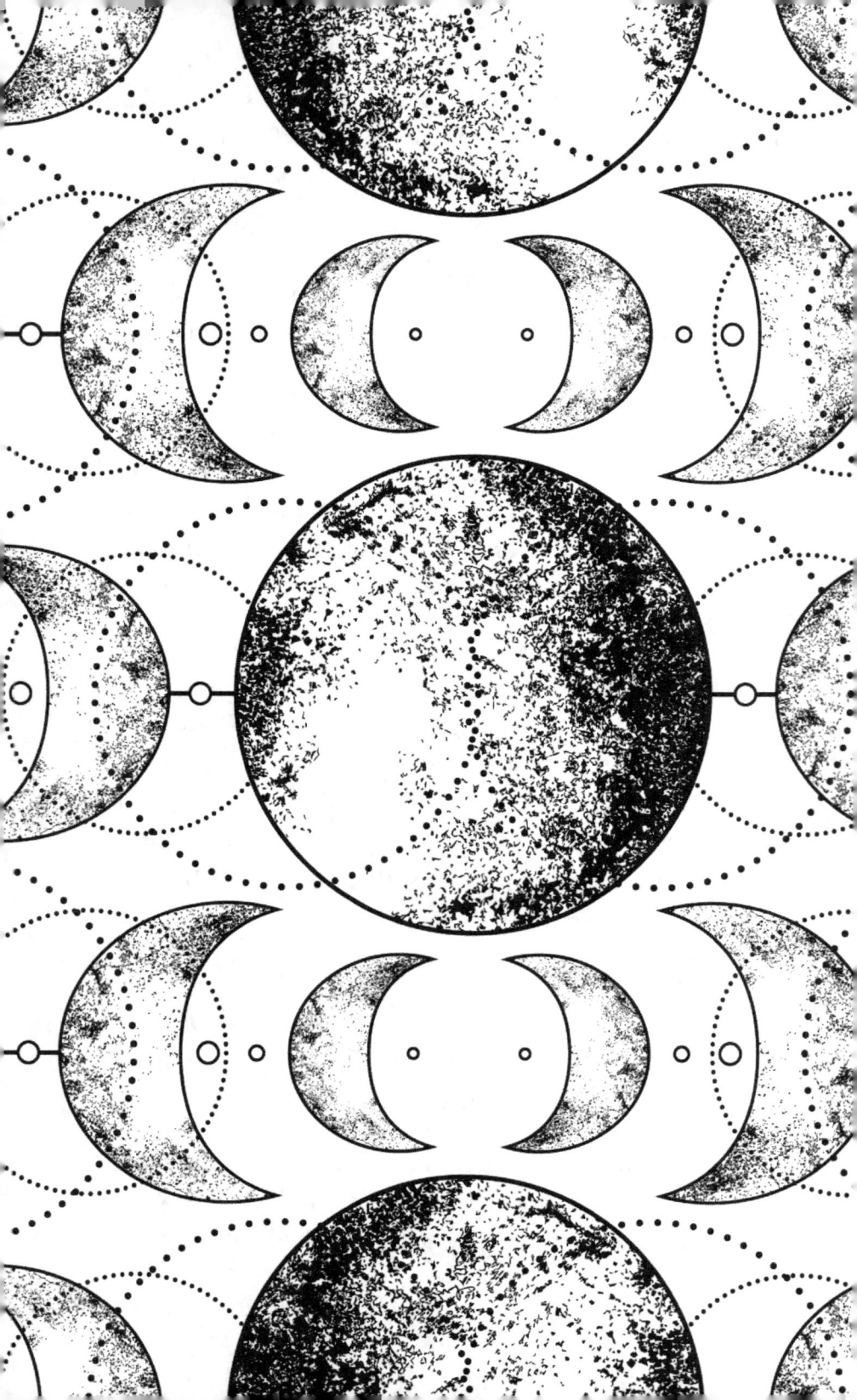

# CHAPTER 19

L arry drove straight through, stopping only twice at rest areas to take a brief nap and grab something to eat. When he crossed the Mexican border into Texas, he considered driving into San Antonio where he knew there was a fairly large airport. He could turn in his rental car there and then fly the rest of the way into Raleigh-Durham. But not knowing for sure if the flight restrictions had been lifted or if he would have to change planes in Charlotte, and thinking it would probably take more time to do that than to just keep driving, he gave up the idea.

It was close to midnight when he pulled into the driveway of the bungalow at Wood Rose. Too tired to bother with unpacking, he got out of the car, stiff from driving so far and fumbling with his keys to unlock the front door. Someone was sitting on the porch steps waiting in the dark. It was Grai.

Recovering from everything that happened, over the next three days Carolina and the F.I.G.s leisurely explored the beautiful grounds full of symbolism and historical richness at the *zhuang yuan*. The koi pond encircled with purple orchids or *Lánhuā*, the meditation garden filled with the

China rose, believed to convey dauntless spirit; chrysanthemum, representing elegance and nobility; and peony, symbolizing riches, prosperity, and honor; and the ruins from one of the earliest Christian churches ever built in China dating back before the seventh century—each tree, each shrub, each flower, and each structure held a special meaning—a special purpose.

Frequently they found themselves drawn to the ancient, square-based pagoda at the far end of one of the many gardens built in 640 during the Tang Dynasty. That was where, on their previous visit, Mackenzie had learned the story of how a young Chinese woman and a man from the far-away country of Scotland fell deeply in love. However, because the Chinese woman's father was head of the ruling family of Qiang, they could not be together; and the child that came as a result of that love was taken away. That was where Mackenzie learned that Ling, the U.S. Senator from Hawaii, was her mother.

Mackenzie remembered everything her mother had told her about the *zhuang yuan* and the generations who had lived there before. They were her family, Mackenzie's mother had told her, and the *zhuang yuan* was her family home.

By the end of the third day, Carolina and her girls were ready to go back to Wood Rose. They would soon return to China, to the land with the ancient poetic name of Cathay—a name that had come from a now-extinct language of the Khitan people, Dara explained to them. But now, they wanted to go home—to Wood Rose. It was time.

The disasters that had occurred around the world

had subsided and were no longer an imminent threat. Everything was returning to normal, at least as normal as it could be. Things once again felt balanced. Carolina and her girls understood why it was necessary to return the key to the cave that was *jinzhi de*, or forbidden, just as Dr. Stanwick did. The world simply wasn't ready yet.

Having rested while staying at the *zhuang yuan*, Carolina felt strong and healthy again. The headache and weakness, the loss of hearing and sight, were no longer there. They had simply vanished. In fact, she felt healthier and stronger than she ever had. She felt renewed.

At some point, late one night, she heard Lyuba's voice, *You did well, my daughter.* Because she was the daughter of a *choovihni*, with the knowledge of gypsies from the beginning of time running through her veins, she knew what Lyuba had done—the sacrifice the mother had offered to the gods in order to save her daughter. And she loved this woman who had given her life all the more for it.

She also had a strong sense that the evil Lyuba had warned her about was still present. And although the evil was weakened, she knew she would need to be mindful of it.

Before leaving, Dr. Stanwick contacted Carolina and the F.I.G.s to let them know the Department of Regional Antiquities and Archaeological Studies in Puli had approved a small grant for the Luoli Project. Dr. Stanwick would continue to search for artifacts at the site, proving that early gypsies had originally settled in that area near the Yellow Sea before traveling into Europe. Those findings would be significant. He would take to his death, however, what he knew about the *jinzhi de* cave, the ancient pig dragon, and the secret it held. That would be his greatest contribution to archaeology. It would eventually become his legacy.

When the four women arrived back at the Raleigh-Durham airport, they were greeted by a smiling and much relieved Larry holding up a big sign welcoming Carolina and the F.I.G.s home. They had been separated for much too long.

Standing next to him with a big smile, also relieved, and also holding up a big sign of welcome and offering his support any way that he could was Larry's good friend, Grai. He had driven his taxi straight through to Raleigh from Mrs. Killebrew's boarding house as soon as he got off the phone from talking to Larry.

As a gypsy and Larry's closest friend, he knew the severe negative implications of what Larry faced. There were very few gypsies and certainly not any settlers who could possibly understand the gravity of what was taking place, and the enormous responsibility that had been placed on Carolina and the F.I.G.s. Not to be with his friend during this dangerous, life-threatening time wasn't even a consideration.

Even though these two men no longer followed the gypsy traditions, they were still gypsies by birth. Because of that, theirs was a special friendship, and it always would be. The lessons they had been taught by their *choovihni* were embedded in them and part of their DNA, and it was those lessons that they would always fall back on in times of need. They understood what it meant for the key to be removed before its time, and how perilous and near the factor of evil was to Carolina and her girls. They knew all too well the tremendous danger Carolina and the F.I.G.s had faced, and how frighteningly close they had come to death.

Grai would spend one more night at Wood Rose and then leave to drive back to New York City early the next morning. After that, Carolina and Larry would take the F.I.G.s to the Raleigh-Durham Airport to catch their early afternoon flights. It was time for them to return to the universities and complete their projects.

That evening, Carolina and Larry hosted a formal dinner party for their cherished and much-loved friends— their first social occasion in their new three-bedroom bungalow. Grai was there and, of course, Dara, Mackenzie, and Jennifer. And Lilian Ball and Edna Grace Alcott. Naturally, there couldn't be a dinner party without Headmaster Thurgood Harcourt and Jimmy Bob Doake.

Each and every one of these people had become an important part in Carolina's life and in the lives of the three females of intellectual genius. They were connected in so many ways and on so many levels. She knew she would never be able to thank them properly, but she could at least invite them to dinner.

She served them a gypsy pot roast from her mother's special recipe that called for cinnamon, a spice obtained from the inner tree bark of *Cinnamomum* that had been used for thousands of years. And, of course, Carolina used the beautiful china and crystal goblets as well as the sterling silver service and stemware that Miss Alcott had given to her. These had been the cherished treasures handed down to Miss Alcott from her mother and grandmother and other members of her family. It pleased Miss Alcott to see her things once again being used, just as it pleased her to see Carolina wearing a beautiful sapphire necklace and matching earrings that she had given to her.

The first to leave were Lilian Ball and Edna Grace Alcott, since it was already well past their bedtime. "Your china, and crystal glasses, and silverware made such a beautiful setting on Carolina's table," Lilian told her friend as they walked arm-in-arm to their bungalow. "Very elegant."

Both Lilian and Edna Grace felt especially light-hearted and joyous after such a pleasant evening. Maybe even a little bit tipsy. "And didn't that bowl of blue hydrangeas make a pretty centerpiece?" She was still thinking about the dinner party and how pretty the table looked. "Carolina said they came from her yard. I wonder what kind of fertilizer she uses?"

Edna Grace was also thinking of the evening's events but her focus was centered in another direction and on another matter entirely. "Did you notice that Thurgood used the wrong fork for the salad?" Edna Grace asked, getting right to the meat of the matter that was on her mind.

"And he dripped sauce on his tie," said Lilian, quickly changing her thoughts from the beautiful table setting.

"And on his pants," added Edna Grace, frowning, and both women broke out into uncontrollable giggles.

Jimmy Bob said his goodnights shortly after the two women left, taking with him a doggy bag for Tick and a kitty bag for Carol and her four kittens that Carolina had prepared especially for his four-legged family. It was almost midnight—time for him to make his security rounds on the Wood Rose campus.

Normally, he did his rounds in his old beat-up truck starting with the outer perimeter along the ivy-covered stone walls surrounding the campus, and then gradually circling his way toward the middle of the large, wooded property until finally reaching the center where the administration building was located.

Without fail, the entire process took him two hours and forty-three minutes unless one of his favorite teams was playing on television—it didn't matter which sport. Then he would only patrol around the dormitory and the administration building, which would take fifteen minutes.

Since there had never been any reason to change this routine, the time he would start patrol was always the same: 12 midnight. And because Jimmy Bob was a bit of a poet, often spending his solitary nocturnal hours transferring his innermost thoughts onto paper while others slept, he visualized himself as heroic, charged with the weighty responsibility of keeping all safe during those hours he referred to in meter and rhyme as "witches' moments"—the magical time that occurs between late darkness and early light.

After dropping off the bags of goodies at his bungalow, Jimmy Bob got into his truck to begin his rounds.

He would make an exception on this night and just do the short rounds even though none of his favorite teams was on television. Ms. Lovel had served wine with her gypsy roast, and it had slightly gone to his head since he wasn't used to drinking wine.

Once in his truck, however, he decided to make another, different exception, and that was to create a new, even shorter, route. He soon confirmed that there was nothing of a threatening nature on the Wood Rose campus and, in no time, Jimmy Bob was back at his bungalow, in bed, and sound asleep.

Headmaster Harcourt felt especially jovial when he returned to his bungalow. He had enjoyed the stories that Grai and Larry told of growing up in a gypsy camp and hearing about all of their travels. And the food and wine was excellent, in his opinion. Such a welcomed change from the bologna sandwiches he had been fixing for himself to eat in his wife's absence. He would have much to tell his wife when she returned. Maybe Carolina would give her the recipe for that pot roast.

The F.I.G.s were the last to leave, having stayed to help Carolina and Larry clean up. As the three females of intellectual genius walked back to their forever home, they were quiet—introspective—thinking about the next day and feeling the stress of having to once again leave Wood Rose and be apart from one another and from Carolina.

"*Shekoo, baboo!*"

"What is it?" Jennifer asked Dara, flipping her ponytail.

Mackenzie nervously ran her fingers through her short brown hair and looked at her friends.

"I am suddenly feeling the urge to create," said Dara.

Mackenzie giggled, and then got very serious. "Are you sure, Dara?"

But Dara was already striding toward the dormitory, and Jennifer was following right behind her.

Within minutes, the three females of intellectual genius had crawled into the dormitory basement through a window. In a few more minutes, they departed the basement the same way they had entered, dragging with them a cot—the one with the bent frame.

Stone apparitions—familiar and functional in daylight—now seemed unfamiliar and a little ghostly in the soft illumination of the crescent moon high overhead; and everywhere dark, elongated shadows crisscrossed the lawn dampened by night-cooled air. The stillness was broken only by the rhythmic croaking of frogs from a nearby pond, an occasional splash, a mocking bird off in the distance, and the slight rustle of leaves—and the sound of suppressed laughter.

When they reached the Administration Building, Dara jiggled the door knob, turned it to the left, then to the right, and lifted. As it always had in the past, the locked door opened. The three young women marched into Thurgood's office where they pushed the soft overstuffed green velvet sofa out of the way and replaced it with a misaligned, lopsided cot.

The sofa required a bit more work, and heavy lifting, but they eventually managed to get it through the Headmaster's office door, out of the Administration Building, hauled across the dew-moistened grass, and shoved up the steps onto the front porch of Jimmy Bob's bungalow. Immediately Tick, the brave guard dog of Wood Rose, jumped up on the sofa covered in soft green velvet and stretched out. Having already enjoyed tasty bites of gypsy pot roast, and feeling like he was such a good dog, he now made himself quite comfortable on his new bed.

Satisfied with their expression of creativity, the three females of intellectual genius went home—to their forever home.

Within minutes after going to bed, Mackenzie tiptoed into Dara's room and stood quietly by the side of her bed.

"Get in," said Dara.

Mackenzie carefully pulled back the neatly folded covers trying not to wrinkle them, climbed in next to another female of intellectual genius, and stuck her foot out from under the covers like a barometer.

A few minutes later, Jennifer stomped into Dara's room, flipped her blond ponytail, and stood at the foot of her bed.

"Come on," said Dara.

Once settled, the three young women stared into the darkness, unable to sleep, not ready to turn off their thoughts and settle their minds. Not yet.

"I saw it, too," whispered Mackenzie. "The portal." Stumbling on the word "portal" the words were soft, almost apologetic, like a confession.

"I know," said Dara. "We all saw it."

"It's all right," said Jennifer. "It is a good thing."

The weighty issue had been discussed, and a new level of understanding as to who they were and why they were so different had been reached. The brilliant minds of three females of intellectual genius could now at last relax, and within minutes, they went into a deep, peaceful sleep— the sleep of innocent angels.

In the stillness of the night, in a bungalow just down a ways, all of the china, silver, and crystal glasses from the festive dinner party carefully washed and put away, Carolina went over in her mind everything that happened that evening and all that had taken place before. She now knew that she and her girls would always feel stressed whenever they were separated from one another. They were Carolina and the F.I.G.s, with a bond that was so unique and so strong that it was impossible to feel any semblance of comfort when they were apart from one another.

Carolina also knew that there would always be other difficulties to face and unimaginable challenges to solve, many if not all of them dangerous. It was their destiny, and they had been brought together for that very reason. Carolina knew these things because she had also glimpsed the portal and she had heard the whispers of the gods. In that one brief instant, she saw all that was, all that is, and all that ever will be.

The loving connection between these four young women was something that had been created before they were born, beyond the world they lived in, perhaps in another dimension—maybe even by the gods themselves. They didn't need to understand it. They only had to just accept it for what it was—something rare and wonderful.

They had so much to look forward to, and, for now at least, still a great deal to do.

Dara would finish her report comparing her discoveries of the pictographs she discovered beneath New York City's Grand Central Terminal to her findings at the archaeological site in the Shandong province of China. Then she would return to China where, after a brief visit at the Luoli Project, she would begin work with Dr. Wu and his special team of archaeologists in the Helan Mountain region. It was there that over 6,000 petroglyphs between 3,000 and 10,000 years old had been discovered depicting human figures and animals, and symbols that appeared to be ancient writing.

Mackenzie would return to the campus of MIT to continue her research in her lab, a private laboratory set up specifically for her, on improving the human condition—specifically, the genetic links between humans and plants in disease prevention. Then, after the first of the year, she would resume her work at the Yellow Sea Laboratory in Puli, China, the internationally known medical research company started by Ling's grandfather—Mackenzie's great grandfather.

Jennifer would begin rehearsals for her much antici-pated performance at Carnegie Hall in New York City over Thanksgiving which, according to Andrew Whatley, Direc-tor of Special Events at Carnegie Hall, was already sold out. In addition to *The Nightjar's Promise*, a symphony written in C sharp major in four movements, and her other original music compositions, *The Gypsy Cadence, The Wish Rider,* and *The Clock Flower,* she would now include in the program her latest musical creation, a symphonic poem—*The Seraphim's Song.*

Thanksgiving was only a few weeks away when they would be together again. Of course, it wouldn't be Thanks-giving unless they stayed at Mrs. Killebrew's boarding house while they were in New York.

Carolina and the F.I.G.s looked forward to once again staying at Mrs. Killebrew's, each beautiful wall-pa-pered room decorated with late Victorian furniture, lace curtains, and an eclectic mix of antiques. And Larry would be able to spend time with his friend Grai. Mrs. Killebrew had already informed them that with the help of Grai she was planning another big soiree for all of them - including Miss Alcott, Mrs. Ball, Headmaster Harcourt, and Ling - following Jennifer's performance at Carnegie Hall.

Carolina thought of all of these things, lying in bed next to the man she loved, smiling, and wondering what the next challenge would be—and when. Whatever happened, she knew that she, Dara, Mackenzie, and Jennifer would find a way to face it and find a satisfying resolution. They were, after all, Carolina and the three F.I.G.s. As she drifted off to sleep, images of albums filled with photos carefully identified with purple ink and sealed boxes labeled with the word *PRECIOUS* also written in purple ink filled her dreams.

It would soon be light; and Wood Rose Orphanage and Academy for Young Women would start another day.

Book 1 Chapters 1-3

# The Cadence of Gypsies

# Chapter 1

The gypsy—not old, but beyond her birthing years—
spent the early, pre-dawn hours digging roots in the dark of the
crescent moon, every so often replanting a good piece of a root
to grow next year. The day before she had picked herbs, during
that time when the essential oils are at their strongest, before they
could get evaporated by the midday sun. She had her favorite
place where she searched, the place where the energies were
strongest. Surprisingly, it was the old church graveyard built on a
slight mound just outside of the rural Italian village of Frascati.
A creek ran nearby, and a tall, unkempt yew tree grew near the
entrance to the graveyard, poisonous, but giving off positive
energies. It was a place she knew well, having discovered it from
a previous time the travelers came this way.

Other gypsy women picked their herbs anywhere they
were found, or they would buy them dried from a shop, claiming
good results. But *Kaulo Camio*, a black gypsy who went by the
name of Lyuba, knew better. To capture their full spiritual
healing essence, she treated all plants kindly and with respect.
For she believed as good gypsies did that everything has a spirit,
even the stones on the ground, and everything could bring
luck—good or bad.

Once she had gathered her herbs, she returned to camp
just beyond the village to prepare her potions. From the roots,
bark, and hard seeds she would make decoctions by soaking
them overnight and boiling them the next day. To some of the
decoctions, she would add honey or sugar; to others she would

thicken into syrup or add lard to make ointments and salves. She saved the freshest herbs for her oils.

Soon her potions would be ready, and she would take them into the village to sell. Coughs or colds, rheumatism, cuts and bruises, burns—it didn't matter. She knew how to relieve pain, create lustrous hair, revive the impotent, whiten teeth, cure constipation, or simply heal the broken spirit. Unlike others who only pretended, she had the gift.

But that would be tomorrow. Today, after her work was complete, she would teach the children. Lyuba was a *choovihni*, a wisewoman, an exalted and envied position among gypsy women. As her birthright, she alone was given the responsibility to pass on the knowledge of the travelers to the ones who would follow. Today she would teach the older children about spells, making the *duk rak* and *duk koor* for protection, as well as the talisman. This particular group of children was bright and eager, but she had yet to find a child born with the natural gift. Those children were rare. In all her years as a *choovihni*, she had only known one—the beautiful one that was taken from her so long ago. All of the magic she knew could not heal her pain from that loss.

Outside her hut, the shadow of the elm was short; the sun almost directly overhead. She needed to finish for soon it would be time for the children. She carefully placed the last of the herbs in a bottle and covered them with olive oil. Sealing the bottle tightly with a cork, she put it with the others where it would be gently warmed by the sun.

* * *

Jimmy Bob Doake didn't like change. Born and reared in Piedmont, North Carolina, and the only sibling out of eleven to make it to the eighth grade, he never felt a desire to visit or move to anywhere else. He still lived in the house where he grew up, at least during the day, alone, except for his hound dog, old Tick. He spent his nights only a couple of miles down the road at the Wood Rose Orphanage and Academy for Young Women, his place of employment for the past 30 years. This night was no different.

Jimmy Bob slowly made the rounds in his old beat-up truck, starting with the outer perimeter along the ivy-covered stone walls surrounding the campus. He gradually circled his way toward the middle of the large, wooded property until finally reaching the center where the administration building was located. Without fail, the entire process took him two hours and 43 minutes. However, on those nights when his favorite team was playing on television—it didn't matter which sport—he would only patrol around the dormitory and the administration building, which would take 15 minutes.

Since there had never been any reason to change this routine, he would always leave his office to go on patrol at midnight. And because Jimmy Bob was a bit of a poet, often spending his solitary nocturnal hours transferring his inner-most thoughts onto paper while others slept, he visualized himself as heroic, charged with the weighty responsibility of keeping all safe during those hours he referred to in meter and rhyme as "witches' moments"—the magical time that occurs between late darkness and early light.

Stone apparitions, familiar and functional in daylight, now seemed unfamiliar and somewhat threatening in the soft illumination of the crescent moon high overhead. Everywhere dark, elongated shadows crisscrossed the lawn dampened by night-cooled air. The stillness was broken only by the rhythmic croaking of frogs from a nearby pond, an occasional splash, a mocking bird off in the distance, and the slight rustle of leaves.

Though the favored Durham Bulls had gone into extra innings against the Indianapolis Indians, the minor league baseball game was being televised by the local station in a delayed broadcast, therefore eliminating the need for Jimmy to cut his patrol short this evening. At exactly two hours and 43 minutes after he started his rounds, he parked his truck and entered through the locked door of the administration building, located on the east end. Within minutes he was comfortably reinstalled in his over-sized recliner, positioned in front of the 12-inch television he kept in his small office. It was the top of the 15$^{th}$ inning; the Bulls 6, the Indians 5. The Indians were up to bat. Next to the recliner on a small table was a bag of cheese chips, a canned soft drink, and the pad of paper and pen he kept handy just in case he felt inspired to write something—a word, a phrase, a nice couplet.

All was as it should be.

* * *

"Ouch! You're standing on my fingers!" said the petite girl with a long, blond ponytail. Her nightgown was pulled up between her legs and tied into a knot at her waist to keep it from getting tangled on the limb where she was perched. Somewhere above her the sound of a saw and splintering wood filled the darkness followed by a stream of profanity repeated in several foreign languages for emphasis.

"It doesn't look right. It's supposed to have a rim and a dent," said the heavy-set girl with a slight lisp. She was wearing a nightshirt buttoned at the neck, and clinging to a 12-foot ladder as she pointed the flashlight.

The petite girl with the blond ponytail giggled.

"What do you mean—*dent*? Let me see that picture." The completely hidden, tall black girl aimed her flashlight toward the magazine being thrust upwards through the thick branches in her direction.

"And the top is supposed to be rounded—like a button mushroom," the girl in the nightshirt added, the word "mushroom" sounding more like "muthroom."

"That's because it's circumcised," supplied the girl with the ponytail, as she removed a small twig and a handful of leaves from the magazine.

"*Shekoo, baboo!*" More profanity. "Okay. I know what to do." The tall black girl disappeared back into the upper-most branches of the tall plant that was more tree than bush. After several more minutes, the sawing, crunching, and clipping sounds finally gave way to the more gentle sounds of tiny snips. And then, silence.

"That's it; everybody down."

With the magazine that had been overlooked in the last confiscation wedged firmly under her armpit, the petite girl started the perilous descent first since she was nearest to the ground, followed by the tall black girl. The girl in the nightshirt eased her way down the ladder last, juggling pruning shears, a hand saw, and scissors. Once on the ground, the three girls stood back to admire their work.

"That is one honkin' *Peni erecti*," said the tall girl, causing a fresh explosion of giggles. "Let's get out of here." After quickly rolling down the legs of her pajama bottoms, the tall girl grabbed one end of the ladder and, along with her two friends, lugged it and the other tools back to the shed that housed lawn maintenance equipment. Task accomplished, they returned to their rooms, careful not to disturb the other dorm residents, the floor monitors, their suite-mates and, most important, their slumbering dorm mother, Ms. Larkins. Within minutes they fell into a deep, peaceful sleep—the sleep of innocent angels.

It would soon be light, and Wood Rose Orphanage and Academy for Young Women would start another day.

# Chapter 2

It was always the older ones who felt the need to challenge the ancient gypsy traditions. The children who weren't yet adults, but who felt they were old enough to thwart authority and desire independence.

"I want lots of gold," said Milosh, who had recently turned 17 years old—a man in his opinion. The oldest in the group, soon he would join the adults. "Teach me the spell to make me wealthy."

"You must be careful for what you wish, Milosh." As always, the *choovihni* was patient with her young pupils. "But I shall teach you the spell for attracting material goods." She sat in the shade of the tall elm with her full skirt spread out around her and waited until everyone was quiet and settled before continuing. "First, write down whatever it is you desire on a clean sheet of paper, then place the paper on a small square of green cloth. You must concentrate on it for a few minutes. That might be hard for you, Milosh," she teased. The other students laughed. They liked for Milosh to be put in his place. Just because he was the son of the Bandoleer, it didn't make him better than everyone else, even though he acted like it. He played mean tricks on the younger ones who were too timid and afraid to say anything. "Try to visualize the object before you—the shape, texture, color. Feel pride in owning it, the pleasure you hope it will bring, what you will do with it." She looked at each of her students, making sure they understood. "Then hold the paper to your forehead and say three times: 'I have you, I hold you, I keep you.'

"Fold the paper into the green cloth and tie it with a length of red wool. Tie seven knots into the wool and as you tie each knot, say, 'You are mine, I own you.' Put the green cloth with the paper in a small box, and each day, for seven days, hold the box to your forehead and say three times, 'You are mine, I own you.' After you have done this, put the box away in the back of a drawer."

"Will I have lots of gold if I do that?" Milosh asked.

"It will bring success to those who are patient and deserving," Lyuba answered.

For the next several hours, Lyuba taught the children other spells: the spell using the power of trees, a ritual to cleanse the aura of their individual spaces, the spell for strength. When they got older, she would teach them spells for attracting romance and for keeping a loyal lover. For now, however, she would teach only those things that were appropriate and what they could understand.

When the day's lessons were complete, and the elm's shadow once again lengthened, the parents came for their children. Concerned, Lyuba watched Milosh return to his hut alone. His *chakra*, that point of light indicating the heart, was dark and brown rather than green as it should be. Much was expected of the only son of the Bandoleer. He held promise, but he had much to learn. Unlike his father, he was impatient and quick to judge others. His focus was on material things, and he ignored what was important. There was also a darkness in his spirit; something that could be dangerous if not corrected.

He would go and prepare the paper, wrapped in green cloth and tied with a thread of red wool, and wish for much gold. He had not understood.

\* \* \*

The slight voice tremor was all that was needed, but the deep, audible sigh confirmed what Carolina suspected: she was in for another real ass-chewing. This was her eighth time called into the headmaster's office in the same number of months since she had been teaching at Wood Rose Orphanage and Academy for Young Women. Each time it had been because her girls had either committed a serious infraction of rules or behaved in some inappropriate way, which was unacceptable within the stone walls of Wood Rose.

Her girls, the ones she had been given total responsibility for, called themselves Females of Intellectual Genius, or FIGs. Everyone else, however, called them strange. Never before in the history of Wood Rose had a student even come close to approaching genius status. Certainly not in the time that Dr. Harcourt had been headmaster. Then, within the short span of one week, two seven-year-old children—Dara Roux and Mackenzie Yarborough—were admitted, each from a different family, a different background, and a different part of the country, but each with an intelligence quotient well within the range of genius. Amazingly, several years later, a third student was enrolled. Jennifer Torres's age and scores were comparable to those of the original FIGs. What Wood Rose could do for these gifted girls was now coming to a close, much to the relief of the administration, faculty, and staff. This would be their final year at Wood Rose, for in June—less than six weeks away—they would graduate.

Carolina was still in bed, deep in thought, when the telephone rang. For several days she had been struggling with how best to approach the headmaster. Shortly after getting hired at Wood Rose, she was put in charge of the FIGs. Since then she had tried to devise innovative ways to excite her girls, challenge their intellect, and, most of all, keep them out of trouble. The inherent problems of being different extended beyond their prickly relationship with Wood Rose staff members. The multifaceted difficulties in teaching the FIGs frequently left the faculty with feelings of inferiority and impotency. None of the other residents wanted to be around them either. Only the youngest residents, who didn't yet comprehend the difference between being brilliant and normal, sought the FIGs' attention. This brought about additional struggles of an inner psychological nature. Carolina had tried a variety of approaches, but, obviously, what she had been doing wasn't working. What had stimulated her when she was their age? What mysteries of the universe had intrigued her?

Then she remembered.

She had just turned 18 when she was accepted into the accelerated liberal arts program at the University of North Carolina in Chapel Hill. That summer, in preparation for the fall term, Carolina was assigned an extensive and comprehensive reading list. That was when she made the discovery, and from that day forward, her life and the way she thought of herself had been charted in a veil of mystery and immeasurable conjecture. What if … became her mantra. She felt as though she had been thrust into a parallel universe. Nothing had excited or concerned her more, before or since. It became her own secret research project, something she remained totally committed to—even with a heavy class schedule that would guarantee an early graduation from the university. It was what motivated her to get up every morning and what kept her working late into the night. With each new bit of information, no matter how small or seemingly unimportant, she was pointed in a different direction, to another amazing discovery and thrilling revelation.

The dedication to her search had not diminished in the years since she first made her discovery. In her personal analysis of it, she didn't know what she hoped to accomplish. She only knew she was somehow connected to one of the greatest mysteries in the world by some strange twist of fate. She also recognized that it was her responsibility to seek an outcome, for, in the end, it would define her very existence.

Within three years of being accepted to the university, Carolina graduated *summa cum laude* with a bachelor's degree in liberal arts; and then, because she didn't know what else to do, she earned a master's degree in foreign languages, and a doctorate in psychology. Through it all, the secret remained with her, her special project. Like an invisible companion, she chipped away at the hidden truths. By staying closely associated with the university, she could access research materials that would otherwise be difficult or even impossible to obtain, especially when it involved materials from foreign countries. It was her obsession, consuming all of her spare time between classes, assignments, lab work, and whatever else was necessary to fulfill graduation requirements. It was her best friend.

There was Larry, of course, who was more than a friend. He was the one person she shared everything with and who had been amazingly helpful in her search for the truth. But other than Larry, she didn't have many friends. She certainly did not have the kind of friends she could ever confide in—about this. And the tenuous connection she had felt with her adoptive parents as a child had all but dissolved once she went off to college. Now, there was only the project. The knowledge that it was a part of her sustained her. It was her mission in life, until, abruptly, one day the real world came into focus.

Her adoptive parents had been more than generous when funding her education, but now, "We have retirement to consider," they patiently explained, "and since you are 25 years old with a doctorate degree …" She needed to get a job.

Of course they were right, and Carolina immediately applied for a position with the institution where she had spent the last seven years. Because of her outstanding educational qualifications, she was hired as an assistant professor of psychology with the university, teaching many of the courses she had just completed. Three years later, she learned of a unique employment opportunity at Wood Rose, located 20 miles from Chapel Hill in Raleigh, and without a moment's hesitation she sent in her application and resume. Maybe it was her background and the uncertainty of her origins that made her want to teach at the orphanage. Or maybe, after spending so many years in Chapel Hill, she simply felt the need for change. The only difficult part of her decision: She wouldn't see Larry every day. "But we can talk on the phone," she had told him. "And we'll have weekends." He had said he understood.

Naturally she was hired. She was young, energetic, highly qualified, and trained, and someone, the headmaster hoped, who could handle the FIGs during their final year at Wood Rose. Certainly, no one else could.

With the time-consuming pressures of adjusting to a new job, and the FIGs in particular, and getting familiar with her different surroundings, Carolina's personal research project got put aside, temporarily tucked away like a rare, precious treasure to be rediscovered on another day.

And it was. It was so obvious. The FIGs were the brightest students at Wood Rose; in fact, they were in the top two percent of the entire population, according to their intelligence quotient scores. Each girl had unique qualities and talents that would be perfect for what Carolina had in mind. Although the academic program at Wood Rose was excellent, these girls needed more than the education offered to them, Carolina reasoned. They needed a challenge, especially before they left the protective environment of Wood Rose. Carolina wanted to give them something special they could take with them—something that would be a source of strength to them for the rest of their lives. It was then that Carolina took out her treasure and examined it to make sure she wanted to share it; and, deciding that she did, started putting together a plan.

Considering the many implications, analyzing all of the repercussions, anticipating the negative questions she would receive and her responses, she thought she had worked out all of the details and was just about ready to make an appointment with the headmaster to discuss it. As she lay in bed thinking, the early morning light softly filtered through the newly-hung blue paisley draperies she had recently sewn, and she was reminded of the Robert Browning poem she had always loved:

*The year's at the spring*

*And day's at the morn;*

*Morning's at seven;*

*The hillsides dew-pearled;*

*The lark's on the wing;*

*The snails on the thorn;*

*God's in his heaven—*

*All's right with the world!*

Presenting her plan would be delicate because it meant doing something totally out of the norm for Wood Rose. It meant breaking with routine, and if she had learned anything since arriving at Wood Rose, it was that no one went against the fixed and steadfast regime that had been entrenched at Wood Rose ever since it first opened its doors. But if she approached Dr. Harcourt at just the right time, and could get approval from the board members, and Miss Alcott, of course, perhaps ... Then the phone had rung.

"Ms. Lovel ... I need to see you in my office—immediately." The sigh had followed.

She grabbed her appointment diary, which she kept on the nightstand next to the bed, almost knocking over the small milk glass lamp in her haste, to see if she had forgotten something. It was Sunday and, therefore, no classes were scheduled. There was only the usual routine: a brisk two-mile walk with her girls at 7a.m., followed by showers and dressing, and then breakfast at 8:30. Mandatory chapel services for the student-residents were conducted from 10:00 a.m. until 11:00 a.m.; faculty and staff were also encouraged to attend, but it wasn't required. Carolina chose not to. She preferred to use that time to think of ways to stay at least one step ahead of her three charges. The rest of the day would be spent in the library helping the girls—not that they needed it—finish up their term paper. She had assigned a report on Mary Shelly's motivation and inspiration behind her character of Frankenstein. It was an assignment the FIGs had enjoyed working on together, and they had uncovered some interesting information. When completed, their report would probably be good enough to get published in one of the literary journals. They would take a break at noon for lunch, and again at six o'clock for dinner. Lights were out by 10 a.m., even on the weekends.

A superior academic program, routine, discipline, and the much-maligned dress code—an assortment of required clothing for outer wear, under wear, and sleep wear appropriate for recreation, classrooms, and chapel, which varied only slightly according to the age of the resident—created the foundation on which Wood Rose Orphanage and Academy for Young Women had been built. In 1894, the founding fathers had insisted on it, and from then until now it suited those who financially supported the orphanage.

The Methodist Church was one of the largest supporters, with an annual contribution that more than adequately took care of 35 percent of the administrative costs. A representative from the Methodist Church sat on the Board of Directors along with 11 other members from the community—mostly successful business leaders—whose combined donations totaled another 14 percent. These board members, reverently referred to as the 12 disciples by those who lived and worked at Rose Wood, also organized an annual Christmas fund-raising charity ball. The proceeds were donated to the orphanage for expenses not covered in the budget, such as landscape beautification, or local field trips when deemed appropriate.

In addition, each year Wood Rose was awarded several State grants, which were earmarked for special educational programs. There was also the occasional donation from individuals who wanted to "help the poor little dears."

Finally, there was Miss Edna Grace Alcott, the feisty 87-year-old great niece of Horace Alcott, a tobacco farmer who had originally endowed the orphanage in the late nineteenth century. She contributed the remaining funds necessary to keep Wood Rose running successfully. In recognition of her continued philanthropy and generous spirit, the chapel had been given her family name: Alcott Chapel. A large portrait of Miss Alcott hung next to an equally large portrait of her uncle, both done in oils, in the vestibule above a Queen Ann console table. Centered on the table where it could be observed each Sunday before services was a Waterford crystal vase filled with pink roses, something Miss Alcott had requested since the pink roses complimented the pale pink color of the garment she wore in the portrait. Without fail, these roses were replaced with fresh ones every Saturday morning; another request.

Dr. Thurgood James Harcourt had served as headmaster at Wood Rose for 27 years. During his tenure, enrollment had remained fairly constant, ranging between 38 and 40 residents, as it had since the beginning. Only during the height of the Depression did enrollment skyrocket to more than 100 students. During his first 12 years as headmaster, he proudly maintained the proper image of Wood Rose, which was expected of an institution affiliated with the Methodist Church. Although nothing remarkable occurred during this time, nothing improper occurred either. Then the first two FIGs arrived. Adjustments had to be made; certain challenges met. The newest young residents had difficulty fitting in with the other, already-established residents. Therefore, soon after their arrival the administration determined the FIGs would be happier if their rooms were located near one another in the same suite. An extra floor monitor was also assigned to help watch after the high-spirited girls with exceptional minds. Then there was the ongoing challenge of developing an educational program to meet their intellectual needs. Often this extra work created discontent among the faculty, and feelings of inadequacy.

Negative press, which had never been a problem prior to the girls' arrival, now seemed to be a constant threat. This could result in smaller donations, which would mean the difference between meeting budget needs, or reducing the already limited number of faculty positions.

When the third FIG arrived only a few weeks before Carolina assumed her new post, other adjustments had to be made and different challenges met, causing Dr. Harcourt to question whether it was worth having three intellectually superior residents full of *joie de vivre*. All of his efforts to maintain a positive, dignified image of Wood Rose with the press and the community at large over the years now occasionally took on a carnival atmosphere because of the FIGs.

However, the slightly stooped but otherwise healthy 59-year-old headmaster with gray thinning hair had no desire to retire early. He had managed to keep the reputation of Wood Rose unsullied, and he did so with firmness and decorum. No one was more dedicated or intimately involved in the detailed operations of the orphanage than Dr. Harcourt, and no one took greater interest in its success. The dark gray suites he wore, the conservative gray-striped ties that might give way to a smidgen of maroon on special celebratory occasions, and his stern demeanor were a reflection of the rules of strict discipline and unwavering routine that had been passed down to him from previous headmasters suited his nature.

The way Dr. Harcourt had emphasized each syllable in the word *immediately* when he called Carolina, however, and, of course, that sigh, suggested the routine was going to be changed on this particular Sunday morning, and that "all was not right with the world." The reason undoubtedly being that the three young women Carolina was personally responsible for, her FIGs, had once again done something unbelievably disrespectful, impertinent, unmindful of authority, border-line destructive—and utterly amazing.

# Chapter 3

Milosh prepared the bundle. The single word *gold* was scrawled on a sheet of paper, wrapped in a square of green cloth his mother had given him, and tied with a length of red wool. He rapidly repeated the words, "I have you, I hold you, I keep you," until he grew weary. Lyuba had said he must put the bundle in a box and repeat the words for seven days. He wouldn't wait. Instead, he shoved the bundle to the back of a drawer and went outside. It was getting dark and already the elders were sitting around the campfire. Milosh's friends were seated there as well, just behind the elders in the shadows, where they could listen but not be observed. He sat down next to one of the boys, pushing a younger boy out of his way. The younger boy did not challenge him.

As usual the talk began with incidents that had occurred that day.

"There have been many changes since the last time we passed this way." The Bandoleer opened the conversation.

There were murmurs of agreement. "It is no longer a small village," said one of the women, who had spent the day in Frascati."

"There are more people, but fewer want to buy," said another who had also spent the day trying to sell her services, but had little to show for it.

"We must be patient," said the Bandoleer. "There are many who don't know we are here yet. When they find out, they will want what we have to offer."

Lyuba remained silent. She hadn't wanted to come back to Frascati—not yet. There were too many unhappy memories here. But it hadn't been her decision to make. More often than not they were getting turned away by the settled population. There were fewer places for them to go. Estrangement was causing distrust, and distrust resulted in fear of the travelers. "They are from the lost continent of Atlantis," some of the settlers said. "They are the last of the priestly caste of the old Egyptian religion, forced out by the New Order," said others. There had even been an archaeological study done linking the DNA between present-day European gypsies to the ancient tribes from India. The settled people didn't understand what the gypsies knew: There have been travelers since the beginning of time, and there would be travelers until the end of time, no matter what the *gorgia* believed.

Lyuba had been especially watchful since their arrival, anxious that she might be punished for her actions so long ago. It was the one time she used the dark magic. Even now, after more than 25 years, she didn't regret it. She reached into the fold of her skirt and felt the small stone worn smooth by the river. It had a tiny, natural hole in it; it was her lucky charm. That morning while she had been digging roots, she had made a small offering—a hair pin—in the nearby stream before returning to camp. She asked for the blessing of good fortune in this place that caused her so much pain.

* * *

"It sure didn't take long for him to notice." Jennifer flipped off the hair dryer, quickly brushed her long blond hair, which was still slightly damp, and pulled it back into a ponytail. Dara and Mackenzie were already dressed in uniforms appropriate for Sunday services— dark blue skirts, yellow blouses, black pumps, and blue tights—and were sitting on Jennifer's bed. "What do you think he'll do?" She walked toward the door as she tied a dark blue ribbon around the rubber band holding her hair in place. The other two followed.

"Not much," said Dara. "What can he do? We will be out of here in a few weeks."

"He might decide not to let us graduate," said Mackenzie.

Dara raised her eyebrows. "Not likely. Do you really think Thurgood wants us around any longer than necessary?"

The three girls skipped down the flight of stairs and hurried out of the building. It was just a few minutes past seven when Mrs. Ball, Dr. Harcourt's administrative assistant, had called to tell them the headmaster wanted to see them. They had showered and dressed in record time. No need to make him wait any longer than necessary. Outside they crossed the lawn, ignoring the Do Not Walk On Grass sign, and paused briefly in front of their artistic creation from the night before, silently paying homage—except for Mackenzie who giggled—before entering the administrative building. Mrs. Ball was waiting for them when they got to her office, located just outside of the headmaster's. As before on similar occasions, she provided no verbal or physical indications that would reveal what they were in for.

"You girls may be seated. Dr. Harcourt will be with you momentarily."

The three girls sat in the same chairs they had previously sat in when called to the headmaster's office. Dara sat closest to the wall, both feet firmly planted on the floor, knees together, looking straight ahead. Mackenzie sat next to Dara, pulling at her skirt as she crossed her legs. And Jennifer, turning at an angle toward Mackenzie and Dara, moved her chair ever so slightly, scraping the floor when she did. Mackenzie fluffed her short brown hair and giggled, and then coughed in an attempt to cover up the act of slight injudiciousness. Dara simply continued to stare straight ahead. Mrs. Ball frowned at all three of them and then continued sorting through the paperwork on her desk.

"She has the hots for Thurgood," Dara whispered to the other two.

Once again there was the scrapping of the chair and a spasm of coughing until, under the pointed glare of Mrs. Ball, all became quiet.

\* \* \*

Carolina quickly showered and dressed. As a member of the faculty, she lived within the stone walls of the orphanage property in her own one-bedroom bungalow, something for which she gave thanks every day. Before coming to Wood Rose, she had lived near the university campus in an efficiency apartment with shared walls, shared noises, and shared smells. Now she only had her own walls, her own noises, and her own smells, which were a combination of fresh citrus and herbs, and whatever else was in bloom that she had brought indoors. She loved her little house, and the privacy and independence it afforded, even if it was a bit like living in a fish bowl. After all, there wasn't much distance between the dormitory and the bungalows. On more than one occasion since her arrival to Wood Rose she had sensed she was being spied on. She even thought she saw binoculars poking out of a second-floor dormitory window where the upper-class residents, ages 15 through 18, lived, aimed in her direction.

Still. She took special pride in her bungalow, lovingly decorating each of the small rooms in an Italian provincial style, with happy colors of blue and yellow and splashes of burnt orange. The bungalow had come sparsely furnished, but Carolina, using the sewing machine borrowed from fellow faculty member Dr. Dolores Smythe, an expert in international affairs, geography, and politics, had worked wonders with slip covers and cushions, a few throw rugs and, most recently, draperies for her bedroom.

And outside, on the little plot of land where her house squatted, she added to the boxwood hedges and single camellia bush those things she knew would thrive in the Piedmont soil of North Carolina: daffodil bulbs, azaleas, and forsythia bushes in anticipation of spring;

hydrangeas and pyracanther with its red berries for the hot summers and autumn. It was her own touch, and it gave her bungalow a slightly different appearance from the others; better attended.

Landscaping was something the previous tenant had neglected, either out of laziness or because of other interests. She guessed the latter since she had been quietly informed by one of her colleagues, Dr. Frank Sturdavant, a professor of math, calculus, and statistics, that the man had been released from all duties a short two months after he had been hired. Apparently his lifestyle was in direct opposition to the morals and teachings Wood Rose was trying to instill in its all-female students. This last bit of information had been revealed through a twitching lip and one profound snort.

Carolina owned a white Honda Civic, but she rarely drove her car unless it was to go into town to shop for incidentals such as fabrics for sewing, or a few groceries for those times when she needed a break from cafeteria food, or if she felt the need to explore somewhere beyond the walls, in which case she usually took the FIGs with her. Except for Larry, everything that was both necessary and important in her life existed within the walls of Wood Rose. Her project, of course, was a different matter; its boundaries were still undefined.

The administrative building was an unadorned three-story stone behemoth centered on 60 heavily-wooded acres of donated land. Radiating from the administrative building in a semi-circle, much like the ribs of a fan, were two, two-story buildings, also built of stone. One contained the classrooms accommodating grades one through 12. The other was the dormitory where 38 orphans, ages five to 18, lived. Each floor was divided into several spacious multi-roomed suites, the residents assigned according to class: elementary, grades one through six; middle, grades seven through nine; and high school, grades 10 through 12. Located in perfect juxtaposition between these two buildings and completing the semi-circle, were three, single-story stone buildings that housed the library, the cafeteria, and the infirmary.

Beyond the stone buildings, surrounding the perimeter of the property were various maintenance buildings. And scattered amidst the bucolic, pine-wooded landscape were the individual bungalows where the full-time faculty lived, one of the contractual requirements that went with teaching at Wood Rose. Faculty members had to live on the orphanage property in the housing provided. All staff, however, lived off the orphanage property except for the dorm mother, Ms. Larkins, and the headmaster's secretary, Mrs. Ball. She had moved into her bungalow only a few years earlier, shortly after her husband died, with the full approval of Dr. Harcourt, the Board of Directors, and Miss Alcott.

There were 10 bungalows in all, each constructed in white clapboard with gray slate roofs, with a comfortable layout that gave the on-campus residents the option of cooking in their own kitchens or eating in the cafeteria. Dr. Harcourt and his wife lived in the largest bungalow, of course, which had two bedrooms. Other faculty members with spouses also lived in two-bedroom bungalows, although theirs didn't have as much square footage as the headmaster's or as much landscaping. The single faculty members and Mrs. Ball were given the smallest, one-bedroom bungalows, and Ms. Larkins, a single woman, had a private suite in the dormitory building.

"Did you see it?" Elizabeth Humphry, a professor of English literature, Romance languages, and art history, asked. She practically knocked Carolina down when she rushed out of her bungalow to meet Carolina as she passed.

"See what?"

Elizabeth's eyes widened, emerging above the round, black-framed glasses she wore to correct a bad case of stigmatism and near-sightedness. Shaking her head in disbelief, she hurried back into the safe environment of her bungalow, closing the door with exaggerated determination.

What could they possibly have done now? Even though Dr. Harcourt hadn't revealed his reason for summoning Carolina, it never even occurred to her that it was anything but something her girls had done. Last month, they had wrapped Dr. Harcourt's pristine office in aluminum foil. Everything—pens, sheets of paper, curtains, desk, rugs, telephone—was covered in silver. Even the paperclips piled in the black-veined onyx bowl, a gift from another graduating class, were each individually wrapped. Nothing had escaped.

Punishment had been light, considering it was their latest creative expression, as it was referred to around campus, in a long line of inappropriate, disruptive behavior they had subjected Dr. Harcourt to over the years, probably because he realized they would be graduating and leaving Wood Rose soon. The FIGs were ordered to unwrap everything and then confined to their dorm rooms for two weeks other than going to the cafeteria for meals, or to the chapel for Sunday services, which was pretty much their usual routine anyway.

The month before that it had been the discovery of unauthorized reading material—or, more explicitly, magazines revealing male nudes—in the FIGs' rooms. Contraband of this nature was totally unacceptable, stringently opposed to the morals and teachings at Wood Rose, and an extreme violation of the rules. For that, they had been assigned kitchen duty for two weeks, washing dishes and cleaning up the dining room after each meal. The symbolism in this punishment had not gone unnoticed by the FIGs or Carolina.

There had been many other expressions of creativity over the years, deeds that had been dutifully recorded in the historical archives at Wood Rose, but lately these expressions seemed to have taken on what most of the faculty and staff considered a more menacing tone of a sexual nature.

Carolina hurried along the brick pathway, bordered by late-blooming tulips and early-blooming peonies, which snaked between the library and infirmary toward the administration building. Up ahead she saw several other faculty members, the early-morning walkers and joggers, standing in a group whispering among themselves. They were all facing in the same direction and appeared to be staring at something. Carolina's heart quickened. Though it was the end of April, the temperature made it feel like summer. Even so, Carolina felt a chill. This was not good. She took a deep breath, attempting to prepare herself and get control of her emotions.

As she approached the others, someone noticed her and, like in the biblical story of Moses parting the Red Sea, everyone silently stood aside making room for her to pass. There, in front of the administrative building, or to be more precise, in front of Dr. Harcourt's large, multi-paned window overlooking the grounds, the dormitory and classroom buildings, the library, the cafeteria, the infirmary, the bungalows, and the maintenance buildings beyond, the headmaster's prize red-tip bush, his *Photinia fraseri*, which stood more than 14 feet high and had a circumference of 32 feet wide; the bush that he had personally fertilized and watered, treated for a rare mold disease, nursed back to health from an equally rare fungus, and hand-trimmed weekly since first planting it when he was named headmaster at Wood Rose, was now pruned to a magnificent, perfectly shaped, 14-foot-tall phallic symbol. A few of the red tips had been left at the top, delicately snipped to create the appearance of a slight red blush.

Carolina's first reaction was to laugh. After all, it really was quite amazing. Just the idea of accomplishing such a fete was something to admire. How on earth had they trimmed the top like that? How did they even get up there? But she soon came to her senses; after all, she was being observed by her peers. She had already been introduced to the hidden jealousies, petty competitions, and downright mean-spirited actions of some of the faculty; she couldn't be too careful on how she conducted herself. She hadn't been at Wood Rose as long as the other faculty members, and she could very easily find herself dismissed just as Dr. Frank Sturdavant, the former professor of math, calculus, and statistics, had been for inappropriate behavior. She still might be dismissed if Dr. Harcourt held her responsible for this latest violation against him personally, and Wood Rose in general. Just when she had wanted to discuss her plan with him. There was no doubt as to who had committed the sacrilege, and the timing couldn't have been worse. Not wanting to make matters any more difficult by delaying the inevitable, she made her way unhindered through the heavy double-wooden doors leading to the headmaster's office.

The FIGs were already there, neatly dressed in their uniforms, seated in the three chairs lined up against the far wall, just as they had been arranged for previous infractions. Each of the chairs was touching the other, as though linking them would give the girls additional strength. Only Jennifer's chair was slightly off kilter, not quite in line, but touching nonetheless. Like before, Dr. Harcourt would deal with them after he had dealt with Carolina.

They each looked up expectantly at Carolina when she entered the office. She winked. Then she turned her attention to the sweet scent of lavender and quick, capable movements of Mrs. Lilian Ball, who was transferring some papers from a desk drawer to the file drawer behind her desk. With the last paper properly filed away, Mrs. Ball noticed Carolina and, without saying anything, critically assessed the jogging shorts, t-shirt, and tennis shoes she was wearing. Carolina had brushed her dark, shoulder-length hair after dressing and twisted it up off her neck with a clip, something she usually did whenever she was in a hurry. The look on Mrs. Ball's face made her wish she had done more. Mrs. Ball pursed her lips. "Dr. Harcourt is expecting you. You may go in."

Carolina had been trying to get into Mrs. Ball's good graces ever since arriving at Wood Rose. But for some reason she just couldn't seem to get it right around that woman. Mrs. Ball had been a fixture at Wood Rose even before Dr. Harcourt had been named headmaster. She knew all of its secrets, but Carolina was willing to bet she would never reveal them. Carolina was also willing to bet that if Mrs. Ball didn't like a member of the faculty, Dr. Harcourt didn't either. Carolina's attempt at a confident smile fell a little short as she entered the headmaster's office, which smelled heavily of wood wax and Mrs. Ball. She heard Mrs. Ball close the door firmly behind her.

Mahogany-paneled, thickly-carpeted, and enveloped in dark green fabric, the headmaster's office always made Carolina feel like she should whisper, or maybe bow her head. She wasn't even Catholic, yet she felt the overpowering need to cross herself and kiss her thumb as she had seen others of the Catholic faith do. Perhaps even genuflect. He remained seated behind his desk and didn't expend any energy on small talk.

"I have been more than patient with those girls," Dr. Harcourt said, turning his back to Carolina to face the book-lined wall behind his massive desk. "I have tried to take into consideration the fact that they are ... different, exceptional." This time he spoke toward the sofa that was covered in heavy dark green brocade. "I had even convinced myself—obviously a serious lack in judgment on my part—that by making them your responsibility, these acts of abomination would cease." He shuffled a stack of papers and slammed them down on his desk. "But this is unforgivable!" This was aimed directly at Carolina causing her to flinch. She decided to take the sympathy route.

"Believe me, I understand. I am just so sorry."

He wasn't finished. "I have never seen such a demonstration of insubordination." His breathing was rapid and his face contained a rosy flush not unlike the top of the *Photinia fraseri*, Carolina couldn't fail to notice. She tried another tactic.

"I believe I have read somewhere that it is healthy for large, older bushes to be pruned occasionally. It encourages new growth and keeps them healthy." She smiled weakly.

"Pruned?" He stood up and flailed his arms toward the dark green brocade draperies that flanked the large window now flooded with morning light since the 32-foot girth of leaves and limbs was no longer there to provide shade. "They might as well have dug it up! Burned it! Chopped it down! What were they thinking?" He sat back down, defeated.

This was getting nowhere. Carolina made a quick decision. She would explain her proposal now and just hope that he would agree. At least it would get the FIGs out of his hair, what little there was of it, for a few weeks. Without waiting to be asked, she eased herself down on the edge of the straight-back chair facing Dr. Harcourt's desk, knowing that if she didn't she would probably collapse.

"I think I have a solution. It is educational, it will give Wood Rose a certain amount of international prestige, it might qualify Wood Rose for additional State grants, and it will keep them away from you for the remainder of the term until graduation." When Dr. Harcourt didn't say anything, Carolina continued. After the first 10 minutes and still no response from Dr. Harcourt, she wondered if he was even listening. When she finally finished presenting her case, he stood, leaned forward, and said two words: "Do it!"